KU-451-004

camp CONFIDENTIAL

Jenna's Dilemma

by Melissa J. Morgan

SCHOLASTIC INC.

New York Toronto London Auckland Sydney
Mexico City New Delhi Hong Kong Buenos Aires

No part of this publication may be reproduced,
stored in a retrieval system, or transmitted in any form or by any means,
electronic, mechanical, photocopying, recording, or otherwise,
without written permission of the publisher.
For information regarding permission, write to Grosset & Dunlap, an imprint of
Penguin Putnam Books for Young Readers, a division of Penguin Group (USA) Inc.,
345 Hudson Street, New York, NY 10014.

ISBN 0-439-75675-8

Copyright © 2005 by Grosset & Dunlap. All rights reserved.
Published by Scholastic Inc., 557 Broadway, New York, NY 10012,
by arrangement with Grosset & Dunlap, a division of Penguin Young Readers
Group, (USA). SCHOLASTIC and associated logos are trademarks
and/or registered trademarks of Scholastic Inc.

12 11 10 9 8 7 6 5 4 3 2 1   5 6 7 8 9 10/0

Printed in the U.S.A.   40

First Scholastic printing, May 2005

camp
CONFIDENTIAL

Jenna's Dilemma

chapter ONE

Dear Matt,

Hey, Big Bro! How's everything at science school? Are you bored to death yet? Just kidding. I'm sure you're having the bestest best time of your life, being that you're such a monster science geek. Ha-ha.

Anyway, thanks for the letter and the "Honk If You Love Cheese" bumper sticker. It's perfect for my collection. I have over thirty now, and they're all taped up to the wall above my bunk. All I need is a car to stick them on and I'm all set. But seriously, I know you're worried about me getting into trouble at camp this year, but I swear, so far I've been really good. Well, sort of good. Almost totally good. I've only pulled a couple of pranks, and they were way small. So don't worry. Mom and Dad won't be getting any freak-out phone calls from Dr. Steve. Like you said, I know they don't need that right now.

But you know, if those two didn't want to get any freak-out phone calls in their lives, maybe they should have thought of that before they had four kids, right? Ha-ha.

Okay, gotta go to lunch. Alex is blowing her top because I'm holding up the bunk. Can you say "control freak"? (I mean, she's one of my best friends, but come on. One of these days she's gonna give herself a way-early heart attack.) Anyway,

I don't have much to send in return for the bumper sticker, so I'm enclosing this leaf from one of the Camp Lakeview trees to remind you of the actual fun summers you used to have here before you became Science Boy. (Kidding!)

Love,
Jenna

P.S. I love you, too! But don't let it go to your head.

"Cupcakes for everyone!" Jenna Bloom called out, placing the big, foil-lined box in the center of the creaky bunk floor. She had returned from lunch to find yet another care package from her mom, this one filled with chocolate-on-chocolate cakes, each covered in sprinkles. Her mother had even put in these cardboard divider things she had invented a couple of years ago so each cupcake had its own little compartment, and there was hardly any mess at all. (Except for some icing on the top of the box. Jenna's mom was all about minimal mess.) As soon as Jenna set the box down, all her friends in bunk 3C dropped what they were doing and hit the floor in a circle.

"You know, I've been trying to get you guys to huddle up for ten minutes, and no one listens to me," Julie, the bunk counselor, said. Jenna could tell by her half-smile that she was only pretending to be annoyed as she stood over them. "Are you telling me all I had to do was bribe you with sweets?"

"All you ever have to do is bribe us with sweets," Grace joked. She dropped the book she was reading and quickly wrapped her curly red hair back in a ponytail. "We *never* get good desserts around here unless Jenna's parents send them to us."

It was true. Jenna's mom and dad *had* been responsible for most of the sugar highs in 3C this summer. Jenna was proud and happy that her parents were so popular with her friends.

"I call the one with the most icing!" Chelsea said, leaning over the box until her long blond hair fell forward and almost got stuck in one of the cakes.

"Which one is that?" Valerie asked.

"I don't know yet, but it's mine," Chelsea replied in her ever-bossy way.

"Well, I'm taking this one," Brynn announced, her voice booming. She grabbed a cupcake from the center and licked half the icing off the top. As soon as one was gone, everyone in the circle attacked, laughing and fake-whining over how small or big their choice was.

"Sheesh. It's like they've never seen a cupcake before," Jenna joked to Alex Kim, who was the only girl in the bunch not grabbing for the snacks. "Don't you want one?"

"Nah," Alex said, shrugging one shoulder. "I'm still stuffed from lunch."

Jenna felt her face flush, and she looked away. Alex was the only person who never took her up on her offers of candy bars and cookies whenever her mom and dad sent packages. It was like she thought she was too good for the Blooms' gifts. Jenna didn't get it. She and Alex had both been coming to camp at Lakeview for four years—the longest legacies in the bunk—and they had always been good friends. They both knew more about Lakeview than anyone else, and together they felt kind of like the leaders of the bunk. But as close as they were, there were certain things about Alex that Jenna didn't understand. Like how she was sometimes so blunt—even when what she said might hurt someone's feelings—and she acted like that was the only way to be. And Jenna *really* didn't understand this whole turning-down-chocolate thing.

"You sure?" Jenna asked.

"Yeah. Thanks, anyway," Alex said, smoothing her hand through her short, dark hair.

"More for us, then," Jenna said, diving in. She grabbed a cupcake and sunk her teeth in, savoring the gooey sweetness. Her mom was the best baker in the world.

"Your parents are so cool," Sarah said, taking a napkin from the box to wipe her mouth. She pushed her Boston Red Sox baseball cap up on her forehead a bit so Jenna could actually see her eyes. "They send you, like, two packages a week!"

"Yeah! Like two packages! It's crazy!" Candace put in as she licked some icing off her finger. Short and pale with cropped brown hair, Candace was one of those people who agreed with everything anyone else said. Her parents didn't believe in sweets and only sent her letters, so Candace spent most of her summer at camp eating as much sugar as possible and feeling ill half the time.

"You're so lucky, Jen," Natalie added with a grin. Her cupcake was neatly displayed on the floor in front of her, standing in the center of its wrapper. Clearly, Nat was trying to figure out the best way to dive in without ruining her new tank top. Natalie's clothes were very important to her.

Yeah, really lucky, Jenna thought, her heart squeezing in her chest as she tried to smile. *Double the care packages. Yee-ha*. She didn't even want to think about the real reason she was getting so much mail this year, so she forced herself to ignore it.

"You know, it's really nice how you always share your goodies with the bunk," Julie said, reaching out and tousling Jenna's curly brown hair.

Jenna brushed aside her unhappy thoughts and beamed over the praise. She glanced at Alex, who looked away quickly as if she hadn't noticed. Jenna knew Alex couldn't stand it when anyone else was singled out.

"Well, when you have two brothers and a sister, you kind of have to learn to share," Jenna said, earning a laugh from her friends.

"Everyone! Let's thank Jenna!" Julie announced.

"Thank you, Jenna!" shouted ten half-full mouths. Then everyone fell into a group giggle fit, crumbs flying everywhere. Even Natalie gave up on trying to stay neat and took a huge bite of her cupcake, letting the sprinkles fall all over the place.

"All right! So now that I've got you all in one place, I have the list of electives!" Julie announced, tucking her short blond hair behind her ears. She pulled out her ever-present clipboard and sat down on Natalie's bunk.

Jenna's heart thumped with excitement. Every two weeks at Camp Lakeview, the campers got to concentrate on two elective programs. Last week, they had given Julie their top three choices, and now they would find out which two classes they had been placed in. Jenna was hoping for photography and sports. She had always wanted to learn how to take good pictures of her friends (and maybe how to take some secret, spy cam–style shots of her brothers and sister as well—very useful for bribery). Plus, sports was always a top choice. Jenna had a lot of extra energy to expend, and she loved all kinds of athletics. She, Alex, and Sarah were the biggest jocks in the cabin, and they always signed up for sports.

"So, Nat, going for nature again?" Jenna teased, nudging her friend as Jessie—the camper who always had her nose in a book—went up to Julie to get her electives.

"I don't *think* so," Natalie replied, flipping her long, dark hair behind her shoulder. "The whole campout thing is a great story, but I *so* don't need to go there again. I'm hoping for the newspaper and ceramics."

"Ceramics?" Alyssa asked, looking surprised. Alyssa was an artist, writer, and all-around creative type. Half her clothes were spattered with paint, and she was always doing cool and creative things with her dark hair, like twisting it into tiny braids or crazy buns. Jenna knew Alyssa had requested arts and crafts and the newspaper as her top electives.

"What? I could be artistic and not even know it," Natalie replied. "This time next year I could have a line of high-end vases and bowls in all the best boutiques in New York."

Jenna, Alyssa, and Valerie, another of Jenna's longtime camp friends, all cracked up laughing.

"Fine! See if I invite you to my red-carpet gallery opening," Natalie grumbled, hiding a smile.

"Maybe she wants to make a ceramic statue of *Simon!*" Jenna teased, watching Natalie's face go red. Everyone laughed even harder, and Jenna giggled happily. She loved making people laugh, and this joke was too easy to make. Simon was a boy in Jenna's twin brother Adam's bunk whom Natalie had been crushing on since the first week of camp. Most of the girls in the bunk thought boys were gross and annoying, so they loved to tease Natalie about Simon.

"Okay, okay. Are you guys ever going to stop picking on me about this?" Natalie asked, still smiling.

"Sometime, maybe," Jenna said. "Check back with me next summer."

"Nat! You're up!" Julie called.

"Ha-ha," Natalie said, nudging Jenna's leg with her toe as she got up and walked over to Julie.

Jenna kicked back and munched on her cupcake while the rest of the bunk went up one by one to get their electives. Suddenly, the door banged open and in walked Marissa, her CIT, along with Jenna's older sister, Stephanie, who was also a CIT. Stephanie had been stuck with bunk 3A, who happened to be the rivals of bunk 3C. Normally, CITs would at least be semi-cold to the CITs of their rival bunks, but not Marissa. She and Stephanie were best friends and couldn't care less about the rivalry.

"Hey, Boo," Stephanie said. "You got cupcakes, too, huh?"

"Steph, I told you not to call me that here," Jenna said, scrambling to her feet. At home, her family nickname didn't bother her, but the last thing she wanted was for her bunkmates to start using the cutesy name for her. Then the guys would find out, and suddenly everyone at Lakeview would be calling her "Boo," which was only her nickname because she had apparently loved peekaboo so much when she was, like, two.

"Oh, right. Sorry," Stephanie said, reaching out to smooth Jenna's hair behind her ears. "God, did you even wash up today?" The girl actually licked her finger and went to wipe something off Jenna's cheek.

"Ew! Do not touch me with that!" Jenna pulled away, her face turning beet red as a couple of her bunkmates giggled. "Okay, *why* did you bring her here?" Jenna asked Marissa.

"I'm not getting in the middle of this," Marissa replied, backing away.

It wasn't like Jenna hated her big sister. She actually loved her—most of the time. But when they were away at camp, Stephanie always acted like she was suddenly supposed to be Jenna's mom or something. And she was only sixteen—just five years older than Jenna. It drove Jenna up the wall. It also didn't help that Stephanie was totally gorgeous and cool, which meant all the girls looked up to her, and all the boys followed her around like puppy dogs. Totally sickening, if you asked Jenna.

"Sorry!" Stephanie said, her blue eyes sparkling as she raised her hands in surrender. "I just came by to borrow some nail polish from Marissa. Pretend I'm not even here."

Marissa and Stephanie walked over to Marissa's bed and started to go through the CIT's big pink box of cosmetics. Jenna let out a sigh. Sometimes it was cool having her sister and Adam at camp with her at the same time. It was nice having family around and knowing there were people she could go to if she needed someone or got homesick. But those things hardly ever happened to Jenna, and in the meantime it was like everywhere she went, there was a sibling watching her or picking on her or trying to tell her what to do. Plus, because her oldest brother Matt had also gone to Lakeview, half the grown-ups here couldn't keep all the Bloom kids straight, so they just called her "Bloom." It was totally annoying. Sometimes she just wished she could get away from them all.

"Jenna, you're next," Julie said.

Jenna quickly wiped her cheek, wondering what Stephanie had seen on there, and sat down next to Julie.

"Okay, you got photography, which was your first choice," Julie told her. "But for your other elective, I could only get you your third choice, the newspaper."

"No sports?" Jenna asked, disappointed.

"No, not this time," Julie said. "But don't worry. You still have a million active activities to keep you busy. And, hey, Natalie and Alyssa are on the paper, so that'll be cool."

"Yeah. Welcome to our world," Alyssa said with a smile, overhearing.

"Cool," Jenna said, brightening.

Since camp had started two weeks ago, she had really gotten to know and like the two new girls. It might be fun working on the paper with them. Besides, she liked hanging out with newbies. Jenna had been coming to Lakeview for years, and the new kids always needed her help finding their way around. It made her feel important. Instantly, her disappointment was forgotten. Jenna had never been one to dwell very long on the bad. She was all about the good. And, besides, Julie was right: They had swimming every day—either lessons or free swim, which was the best part of camp. Plus, the bunk competed in various sports with other bunks in their age group almost every day. She would have plenty of exercise.

"So, Bo . . . I mean, Jenna," Stephanie said, stepping up with a bottle of silver nail polish. "What did you get?"

"The newspaper and photography," Jenna replied.

"Oh, that's so cool!" Stephanie exclaimed. "I just saw Adam before I came over here, and he got photography, too! I guess you guys will be spending a lot of time together!"

Jenna tipped her head back and groaned. Perfect. So much for getting away from her family. Two whole weeks stuck in the darkroom with her twin brother. Wasn't it enough that they'd had to share a womb for nine months? When was the torture going to end?

chapter
TWO

That night in the mess hall, everyone was even rowdier than usual. There was a rumor going through camp that there was going to be some big announcement, and all the campers were buzzing, wondering what it might be. Voices and laughter bounced off the wooden rafters high above, filling the room with a crazy mix of happy noise. It was so loud, Jenna swore she could even see the cobweb-covered lights swinging on their wires overhead.

"What do you think the big news is gonna be?" Karen asked Jenna excitedly, digging into the orange sherbet that the kitchen staff passed off as dessert. Usually, Karen was the shyest girl in the bunk. She kept to herself during free period and barely spoke at meals—or ever—but even she couldn't help but be affected by the excitement in the air.

"It's going to be a dance," Alex said, cutting in before Jenna could answer. "It's *always* some kind of dance."

"Really?" Natalie asked, leaning forward in her seat. "That could be cool!"

"Yeah, they actually are," Jenna said, eager to

share her Lakeview info. "They usually have all these great decorations and crazy amounts of snacks, and everyone gets all dressed up."

"Well, as dressed up as you *can* get around here," Grace put in. "I've been saving my favorite rhinestone barrette just in case," she added with a grin. "Last year, I had *nothing* cool to wear."

"Well, my mom called ahead to see what I would need, and when she found out about the yearly dance she bought me a new sundress," Chelsea said, tossing her blond hair back. "I haven't even cut the tags off yet."

Jenna caught Alex's eye, and they both stifled a groan. Chelsea was new this year, and they had found out early on that she was smart and funny. But she could also be a bully and was totally into her looks. Plus, she *loved* to show off.

"This is so beyond cool," Natalie said. "I brought all kinds of stuff that I never thought I'd get to wear once I got here. Like my new denim miniskirt and that purple tank top with the appliqué flowers . . . I'm going to have to do some serious outfit planning."

"Well, I have no dance-worthy clothes," Alyssa said. "Who knew they had dances at camp?"

"You can borrow something of mine, if you want," Natalie offered. "So, do people have, like, dates for this dance?"

Please! Dates? Jenna thought. *I'd rather eat all the leftover sloppy joe surprise!*

"Some of the older kids ask each other," Alex said. "But I don't think anyone in our year will."

"Oh," Natalie said, her face falling.

"Why? Did you want *Simon* to ask you?" Jenna asked. "Natalie and Simon sitting in a tree! K-I-S-S-I-N-G!"

She glanced over at Simon and Adam's table and found them and a bunch of their friends trying to get their spoons to stick to the ends of their noses. Adam's spoon clattered to the table, and they all cracked up laughing. "What do you see in them, anyway? They're such losers," Jenna said.

"But cute losers," Chelsea put in, raising one eyebrow.

Jenna stuck her finger in her mouth to fake gag. Two weeks ago, Chelsea had claimed to be just as grossed out by the boys as the rest of them, but clearly that was a big fake out. Lately it had become obvious that she was almost as boy-crazy as Natalie.

"I just hope none of you think my brother is cute," Jenna said, pushing away from the table. "Because that would just give me nightmares."

"You're going over there, aren't you?" Natalie asked as Jenna stood up.

"Yep. I have to talk to my evil twin," Jenna replied.

"Tell me if Simon says anything about me?" Natalie begged.

Jenna tried not to roll her eyes. "No problem," she replied.

"Uh, Jenna? Where are you going?" Julie asked, sounding worried.

"To talk to my brother," Jenna replied.

"To talk to him? Not to pull some prank on him?" Julie asked.

Jenna smiled. "No, Julie, I swear." She crossed her heart with her pinkie for good measure.

"Okay, then!" Julie said with a smile, though she still looked doubtful.

Wow. Pull a few lousy pranks and one raid and nobody trusts you anymore, Jenna thought. *Well, one raid each summer. Maybe two.* She walked over to Adam's table and dropped down into a chair next to him.

"Jenna? What are you doing over here?" Adam's bunk counselor Nate asked, with an expression that looked a lot like Julie's just had.

"I'm not pulling a prank!" Jenna half-shouted.

"Like you could really pull one over on us," Adam said.

"Hello? I've only done it, like, a million times before!" Jenna reminded him.

"But not tonight," Nate said.

Jenna rolled her eyes. "Not tonight. I promise," she told Nate. She turned to her brother while the rest of the guys continued their stunning spoon tricks. "So, Adam, we need to talk."

"I know," he said. "Did you get the cupcakes from Mom today?"

Jenna's heart turned over in her chest. "Yeah, but that's—"

"Unbelievable, right? I mean, it's like they're trying to bribe us or something. I didn't even finish the candy Dad sent over the weekend yet," Adam said, looking down.

Jenna did not like the way this conversation was going. "Yeah, well, that's because you don't share," she said. "So listen, do you really *have* to take photography?"

"Photography?" Adam asked, blinking. "That's why you came over here? I thought you wanted to talk about—"

"Yeah. I want you to drop it," Jenna said, cutting

20

him off. "Drop photography and take something else."

Adam sat up straight in his chair, and she knew she finally had his full attention. "Why?"

"Because I'm taking photography. And, you and me? We can't be in the same elective at the same time," Jenna said.

"Why not?" Adam asked.

"Because! You . . . you . . ." And that was when Jenna realized she didn't have a real reason. What was she supposed to say? *"I don't want you around me?"* Adam had thick skin, but even he would probably be upset by that. It didn't even really make sense to her, but it was how she felt.

"Because I what?" Adam asked.

"Because you smell!" Jenna said, blurting out the first thing that came to her mind.

All of Adam's friends cracked up, and her brother's face fell. For a split second Jenna felt beyond awful. She couldn't believe she had just made fun of her brother like that in front of everyone. But then his face broke into his silly, wide grin. He lifted his arm and took a huge, long whiff of his T-shirt at the armpit.

"Ugh!" Jenna groaned, along with some of the guys.

"Fresh as a flower patch," Adam said, picking up his spoon and digging into his dessert. "Sorry, sis, but if you want to avoid me, *you're* gonna have to drop photography. You'd better get back to your friends. I'm sure you're missing some very important lip-gloss tips or something."

All the boys cracked up laughing, and Jenna felt her skin turn blotchy and red. She stood up and stalked back to her table, humiliated. She knew it was a little jerky to ask Adam to quit photography, but she just wanted one thing to herself. Why couldn't she have been an only child? Or, at the very least, the only one born on her birthday?

▲ ▲ ▲

"All right, everyone! Settle down, settle down."

Dr. Steve stood in front of the microphone at the front of the room next to the long table where the camp directors and coordinators ate. An excited twitter raced through the mess hall.

"This is it! The big announcement!" Grace said with a grin. She pulled her legs up and tucked them under her to give her added height so she could see better. Ever positive and always up for fun, Grace had a way of getting excited about everything—even Dr. Steve's unsurprising announcements.

The camp director was a tall man with thinning blond hair and a high forehead. His face was constantly pink because, no matter how much sunblock he wore, he always seemed to burn. During the day, he was always seen in a fisherman's hat, shorts, and a white Camp Lakeview polo. But at dinner, he wore khaki pants and a dark blue Camp Lakeview polo. He had worn this uniform every single night since the beginning of time. Even Jenna's older brother Matt had confirmed this. In fact, Matt had asked Jenna to let him know the first time Dr. Steve changed his outfit, because Matt would have to throw a party to celebrate the event.

Dr. Steve tapped at the mike. He tried to shush

the campers with a few dozen "shhhs" and "ahems," but it wasn't until a huge peel of feedback split the room that everyone finally shut up.

"Thank you," Dr. Steve said, blinking rapidly as he leaned toward the mike. Jenna glanced at Alex, and they shared a smile. They had noticed Dr. Steve's crazy blinking habit their first summer at Lakeview, and Alex had come up with the nickname "Dr. Flutter Bug." Ever since then, neither of them could see him without thinking of it.

"First off, I'd like to remind everyone that Visiting Day is in just two weeks," Dr. Steve announced.

The entire room exploded in a roar of cheers and applause, and Grace even threw her fists in the air as she whooped. Everyone loved when their parents came to visit, no matter how embarrassing they were. Visiting Day meant three things: tons of food, clean clothes, and lots of presents.

As Dr. Steve tried to get the room to "settle down" once more, Jenna picked up her spoon and dipped it into the orange soup her dessert had become. She lifted it and stared as the goo dripped off the end and back into the bowl. Lift, turn, drip. Lift, turn, drip. It was mesmerizing.

"Jenna? You okay?" Julie asked as the room began to quiet again.

Jenna dropped her spoon with a clatter. "Yeah. Fine. Why?"

"You don't seem too psyched about Visiting Day," Julie pointed out.

"Yeah. Even I can't wait, and my mom's a total freak and my dad's a total flake," Alyssa put in. "At least you know both your parents will show up."

Yeah. Sure. Right, Jenna thought, a pit of sour sadness forming in her stomach. *The perfect Blooms will definitely be here to see all their perfect kids.*

"Everything okay?" Julie asked again.

Jenna opened her mouth to reply, but Dr. Steve tapped the microphone again before she got a word out.

"But before Visiting Day, there is one other event that I think you will all be very excited about," Dr. Steve put in. "The night before Visiting Day, we are going to have . . ."

Jenna saw Natalie cross her fingers. Valerie and Chelsea sat up a little higher in their seats. Grace was beaming so brightly, she could have lit up the entire camp. Even Sarah, the bunk's major jock, who would never even *think* about getting dressed up, looked excited.

"A camp-wide social!" Dr. Steve announced, just as Alex mouthed the words, *"A camp-wide dance."*

Half the room gasped in excitement, and Jenna glanced at Alex.

"Dance, social. What's the difference?" Alex asked.

"What *is* the difference?" Natalie asked.

"Nothing, really," Marissa replied, sitting down at the end of the table with Julie. As a CIT, Marissa also had the job of waitressing at meals, and she always joined the table when her duties were done. "There will still be dancing. They just decided not to call it a dance because the younger kids get all weird about it."

Jenna knew this was true. Every year while all the older girls danced with the older boys, the younger girls stood around and looked awkwardly at the boys across the room. Some kids didn't want to dance at all because they felt silly. Other kids were terrified of asking someone to dance and even more terrified of being asked to dance. A lot of kids got stressed out about it in the days leading up to the event. Of course, Jenna had never been one of them. She just saw the camp dance as a chance to eat snacks and hang with her friends. And she didn't think that using the word "social" was going to fool anyone. They all knew it was still the camp dance.

"We'll be having all kinds of sweets and snacks, and Pete, the assistant cook you all know and love, has graciously offered to deejay the event," Dr. Steve continued.

Pete took a step away from the wall where he had been lounging and threw his fists in the air to loud cheers and hoots from all the guys. Gangly and sweet, Pete was a camp mainstay. Up until this year, he had been a counselor and definitely one of the cooler ones. This summer, he had taken a job in the mess hall, although Jenna had no idea why. Even looking after the boys had to be better than working with the so-called food they served around here.

"A DJ? That's so cool!" Valerie said, her eyes wide.

"I hope he's got some good music," Alyssa put in.

"Last year at the camp-wide dance, they actually played Kenny G.," Grace said, scrunching her face up. "I mean, my *grandmother* listens to Kenny G."

"Who's Kenny G.?" Jessie asked. For the first time, she lifted her nose from the book it had been buried in the whole time she had been eating.

"Exactly!" Grace said, raising a hand. "No one knows! He's, like, this weird old guy with freaky long hair who plays elevator music. I swear he hypnotizes old people into liking him. Oooh! But wouldn't it be so cool if you could hypnotize people into liking you?" she added, her eyes bright.

Jenna and her bunkmates laughed at this latest babble of Grace's. "Don't worry. Everybody already likes you," Jenna assured her, causing her friend to blush under her freckles.

"We would like the campers to be as involved as possible in planning this event," Dr. Steve continued. "After all, this is your party. To that end, we'll be creating a planning committee made up entirely of campers."

Jenna's eyes widened, and she looked from Alex to Brynn to Grace. Now *this* was new. Campers had never been involved in the planning of the annual event before. If Jenna could get on the committee, she could make sure that it was the best social/dance/whatever in the history of Lakeview. And she could help them avoid the classic mistakes. Like Kenny G.!

"This is so cool!" Grace said, clasping her hands together.

"Counselors, we will be taking two volunteers from each cabin. Please bring the names of your volunteers to my office tomorrow morning," Dr. Steve said, shouting now to be heard over the excited chatter. "Thank you for your attention," he said. Then he gave up and sat down at his table again.

"I totally want to be on the planning committee!" Chelsea said instantly.

"Me too!" Jenna put in.

"So do I!" Natalie added. "Don't you, Alyssa?"

"Yeah," Alyssa said. "It could be fun."

The whole table erupted as everyone tried to volunteer for the committee.

"You guys, you can't *all* be on the committee," Julie said, holding her hands up. "Then none of you would get to be surprised on the night of the social."

"And besides, Dr. Steve said there could be only two from each bunk," Brynn added.

"You're right," Alex said, sitting back. "I'm out. I wanna see what the rest of you come up with."

Jenna couldn't have been more surprised if Alex had just unzipped her face and revealed that she was actually an alien. Alex didn't want to be in charge of something? Not possible.

"Yeah, it's okay," Candace put in. "I'm not really into it, anyway."

"Me neither," Karen added.

"I don't have to do it, either, Julie," Jessie offered.

Julie looked at the rest of them expectantly, waiting for more of them to back down, but no one did. "The rest of you want in?" she asked.

The table erupted again as everyone tried to make her case.

"All right! All right!" Julie said, attempting to quiet them. "Like Brynn said, I'm only supposed to submit two names." She picked up her ever-present clipboard from under her chair and tore off a page of blank paper. "I'll write everyone's name down on strips of paper, and then we'll pick—sound fair?"

Natalie and Grace and a few others nodded their approval, but Jenna's heart sank. Her name was *never* pulled out of hats or barrels or bowls. She was just not lucky with those things.

"Sarah? Can I borrow your hat?" Julie asked when she was done tearing paper and writing names.

Sarah pulled off her Red Sox cap, her ponytail flopping through the hole in the back, and handed it to Julie. All the names were dumped in the hat, and then Julie shook it up.

"Alex, since you were the first to gracefully bow out, how about you do the honors?" Julie asked, holding the hat out to Alex, who was sitting to her right.

Alex sat up straight and made a very serious face as she dipped her hand into the hat. Jenna held her breath. Alex unfolded the first strip of paper and held it up for everyone to see. "Chelsea," she said.

"Yes!" Chelsea cheered.

So unfair, Jenna thought. *Why should a newbie get to be on the committee and not me? At least I've been to these things before.*

Julie shook the cap again, and Alex put her hand inside.

Please just say Jenna, please just say Jenna, please just say—

"Jenna!" Alex announced.

"No way!" Jenna blurted, causing everyone to laugh. Alex leaned over to high-five her, and Jenna slapped her friend's hand. She couldn't believe it. Her name had actually been chosen! She was going to be on the planning committee!

"So Chelsea and Jenna will represent us," Julie said, dumping out the rest of the names and handing the hat back to Sarah. The rest of the bunk sat back, disappointed.

"Don't worry, you guys. We'll all come up with ideas, and then Chelsea and I can give them to the committee," Jenna suggested.

Everyone brightened a bit at this plan, and Julie

grinned. "Now that sounds fair, doesn't it?"

"Yeah," Grace replied, chorused by the others. "Thanks, Jenna."

"No problem," Jenna said, her mind already brimming with possibilities. She couldn't wait to put her own personal touch on the camp-wide social. Now all she had to do was figure out what her personal touch would be.

▲ ▲ ▲

"I can't believe Chelsea got picked," Brynn complained as she, Jenna, Alex, and Grace walked back to the bunk together after dinner. "She's a newbie. Julie should have done it by seniority."

"You only think that because I said no, and then you and Jenna would have been after me in line," Alex said.

Jenna, Brynn, and Alex would have been at the same point in line, actually, but Jenna didn't bother to point that out. They all knew it, anyway.

"So?" Brynn said, kicking at a stone on the walkway.

"Don't worry, Brynn. Like I said, if you have any ideas, I'll bring them up at the meetings," Jenna told her.

"Good, because I have about a million," Grace put in, fiddling with her colorful plastic rings. "We could have a fifties theme! You know, like *Grease*? Or like a *Gone with the Wind* theme? Like a Southern ball? Ooh! Or maybe it could be a Mardi Gras theme! I went to Mardi Gras with my aunt and uncle one year, and it was so cool! Well, I didn't get to see a lot of it because I had to go to bed early, but in the morning there were beads *everywhere*."

"Good ideas," Jenna said. "Maybe you should

write them down or something so I remember them."

"Totally!" Grace said, putting a little skip in her walk that made her crazy red curls bounce all around. "I'll do it when we get back."

"Just make sure you give it to Jenna and not Chelsea," Brynn suggested. "I don't trust that girl yet."

"That reminds me," Alex said, walking backward to look at Jenna. She glanced around at the other random campers walking and talking nearby and lowered her voice. "Whatever happened to the initiation prank?"

Jenna blinked. She couldn't believe it. She had entirely forgotten about the initiation prank this year! *Wow. I've been* really *distracted*, she thought.

"Yeah! What about that? You did it to me, Jessie, and Candace last year," Grace said.

"And Val and Sarah and the others two years ago," Brynn added.

"Yeah. Everyone in the bunk who came after us has been a victim at some point," Alex pointed out. "Don't Chelsea, Nat, and Alyssa need to be initiated, too?" she added, raising her eyebrows.

Jenna glanced over her shoulder at Natalie and Alyssa, who were walking with Valerie, Jessie, and Sarah, gabbing about the social. Now that she knew them so well, she wasn't sure she wanted to prank Natalie and Alyssa. They didn't feel as new to her anymore. They were already her friends.

"Maybe I waited too long," Jenna said.

"Hey! Don't wuss out on us," Brynn said. "It's a tradition."

Jenna caught a glimpse of Chelsea now, who was walking with Simon, Eric, and Adam, tossing her hair and flirting. Ew! Flirting with *Adam*? And even worse, Adam was smiling and laughing. He seemed to be *enjoying* it. Maybe some newbies *did* need to be pranked.

"All right," Jenna said, her eyes sparkling with mischief as she turned back to her friends. "Let's do it."

"When?" Alex asked, her dark eyes bright with excitement.

"Why wait?" Jenna said, a skitter of excitement racing over her skin. "Tomorrow we make a plan. And tomorrow night, the newbies get initiated."

chapter

THREE

The next morning, Jenna stood on the edge of the wooden planks that made up the beginner's diving pier at the Lakeview lake. The sky was a gorgeous blue with just a few whispy-white clouds. The sun was hot on her shoulders and all around the lake, campers laughed, splashed, and squealed, having the time of their lives. Across the water, in the deep end, the senior boys and girls were doing relay races while their friends shouted encouragement from the sand. Jenna watched them, wishing she were over there having fun instead of standing over the rippling water, terrified.

In the water below Jenna, Chelsea and Alex dog-paddled, having already made their dives. Behind her were a bunch of other boys and girls in her swim skill level, all gossiping and messing around while they waited their turns. Everyone was happy and relaxed and looking forward to that night's movie-night viewing. Everyone except Jenna.

The water looked so far away. Even though she could probably reach down with her toe and touch the cool surface of the lake, it still looked so far. Was she really supposed to launch herself from the safety of the platform and crash headfirst into the water? What if there was something down there? Like a rock? She could crack her head open and die and her body would sink to the bottom of the lake and no one would ever find her and—

Sometimes having a good imagination really stinks, Jenna thought.

The whole camp was divided up into colors according to their swimming ability. Those who were just learning to swim were reds and had to stay in the shallow end. Those who could swim but weren't experts yet and couldn't dive were yellows, like Jenna. Those who could dive and were practicing for their deep-end swim test were greens. The experts, who had passed the final test and could do it all, were blues.

At the end of last summer, Adam had accelerated right through green and straight to blue, and Jenna had been totally jealous. Not many eleven-year-olds were blues, and it killed her that Adam was so far ahead of her. But staring at the water just then, she felt she wouldn't have minded staying a yellow forever.

"Okay, Jenna, just put your hands together over your head like a V," Tyler Bernal, the swim instructor, told her. He was in the lake, one hand holding onto the ladder to the pier, the other treading water.

Tyler was new to camp this year, and with his curly dark hair, tanned skin, and killer smile, every girl at Lakeview was in love with him—especially Jenna's sister Stephanie. Half the camp was whispering about the possibility that Tyler and Stephanie would be a couple before summer's end. Even Jenna thought Tyler was pretty cool. But if he really made her dive headfirst into this lake, that opinion was going to change.

Jenna did as she was told, but her knees were shaking so violently, they were actually knocking together. This was something Jenna had thought only happened in cartoons.

"Good, now bend forward toward the water," Tyler instructed.

Jenna bent at the waist. She felt like she was going to throw up. This whole feeling was new to Jenna. Normally she wasn't scared of anything.

"Come on, Jenna! You can do it!" Alex called out from the water, clearly sensing her terror.

"Good, now bend your knees a little, tuck your head, and dive," Tyler said.

You make it sound so easy, Jenna thought. *Like I'm not about to die.*

"Okay, Jenna, on the count of three," Tyler prodded gently.

Jenna squeezed her eyes shut. She could hear the first-year campers giggling and splashing at the shallow end of the lake. She could hear the water lapping against the platform. She could hear Tyler counting up.

"One . . ."

I can do this, I can, Jenna told herself. Though her pounding heart didn't seem to agree.

"Two . . ."

I can. I can. I can . . .

"Three!"

Jenna opened her eyes, saw the water, and panicked. She stumbled back from the edge of the platform, and her bare heel caught in one of the grooves between the boards.

Luckily, Grace caught her before she could fall on her butt.

"Are you okay?" Grace asked, pulling off the little nose clip she always wore for swimming.

"I can't," Jenna heard herself say, shaking her head. "I can't do it. I just can't."

Tyler was out of the water in an instant, walking over to her with his red swim trunks dripping all over the planks. "It's okay, Jenna. You don't have to do it today," he said. "We can work on it some more."

"Yeah, don't worry, Jenna. You don't have to do it today," Candace said, repeating Tyler's words like she always repeated everyone's. "It's no big deal."

"Remember last year? It took me, like, forever before I could even put my head under the water," Grace reminded her. "I felt like such a total freakazoid! But you were the one who told me to just take my time, and by the end of the summer, I was swimming."

Jenna's heartbeat started to return to normal, and she managed to smile at her friends. They were right. She didn't have to get everything on the first try, did she? Besides, she was the best softball player in the bunk and the best kickball player. She didn't have to be great at *everything*.

Just when she was starting to feel better, Chelsea and Alex stepped up from the ladder.

"Omigosh! You looked hil-*ar*-ious standing up there all shaking," Chelsea said, holding her stomach as she laughed. "I can't believe Jenna Bloom is afraid of diving!"

"Chelsea!" Alex said reprovingly.

Jenna's cheeks reddened in embarrassment.

"You know you're not going to move up to green

if you can't dive—right, Jenna?" Chelsea said. "You'll be stuck in the kiddie end next summer while we're all hanging out over here."

"Like I really want to hang out with you," Jenna shot back. Why did Chelsea have to be so mean? And only some of the time. If she were mean *all* of the time, at least Jenna and the others would always be prepared, but it was like one second she was a completely normal friend and the next second she was being a total jerk.

"All right, girls. That's enough," Tyler said, putting his hands on Chelsea's shoulders and steering her to the back of the line. He rejoined Jenna and crouched next to her. "Check it out," he said, lifting his chin toward the next platform where the diving boards were.

Jenna watched as her brother Adam climbed the five steps to the mid-level board, walked confidently to the edge, and dove off. He barely made a splash when he hit the water. All his buddies and some of the other blues cheered for him when his head popped up again. Even Sarah, who had been in blue forever, and Natalie, who had been put in blue right away after taking her swim test, applauded for him. Adam's grin was practically blinding.

"If your brother can do it, you can do it—right?" Tyler said.

Jenna swallowed hard. There it was again, the Bloom Curse. Now she felt like an even bigger loser because Adam was so far ahead of her. Back when Grace couldn't duck under the water, everyone was patient and cool about it. But now, if Jenna didn't catch up with Adam, everyone would tease her for being so far behind her brother. It was so unfair.

"Want to try it again?" Tyler asked.

Jenna shook her head. "No."

"You sure?" Tyler asked.

"Can't we just do it at the next lesson?" Jenna asked. She crossed her fingers behind her back and added, "I'm sure I'll be ready by then."

"Yeah. I'm sure she'll be ready by then," Candace echoed.

"Okay," Tyler said, standing up again. Jenna felt relieved that he was no longer staring her straight in the eye. "Why don't you sit with your feet in the water while the rest of the campers take their turns? When we're done we'll all go for a swim."

Jenna nodded silently and sat on the edge of the pier. She stared down at the surface of the lake as she swirled her legs around, keeping her back to the diving platform. The last thing she wanted was to have to keep watching her brother show off his skills. For the first time in her life, Jenna couldn't wait for swim period to be over.

▲ ▲ ▲

Jenna sighed as she used her fork to make crisscross designs in her puddle of ketchup. Lunch was almost over, and most of the girls in her bunk were gathered around a new magazine Marissa had gotten in the mail, taking a quiz titled "What's Your Style Personality?" Jenna was so not interested.

"Want my Tater Tots?" Alex asked from the seat across from Jenna.

Jenna eyed the pile of potatoes that were left on her friend's plate. Did this girl never eat? "Sure," she said, pushing her plate toward Alex's. Alex used her fork to shovel the Tots over to Jenna, who promptly drowned them in ketchup.

Alex glanced down the table. Once she seemed convinced that everyone else was occupied, she leaned in toward Jenna. "So, you were really scared this morning, huh?" Alex asked.

Jenna's eyes flashed, but then she looked at her friend and realized she wasn't teasing her. Alex's dark eyes were open and concerned. Jenna looked down at her plate.

"I just don't get how you do it," Jenna said. "I mean, you're *not* scared?"

Alex shrugged one shoulder. "Maybe I was the first time. A little. But once you do it once, it's no big deal."

"Really?" Jenna asked, doubtful.

"Yeah. It's actually fun," Alex said.

Jenna couldn't believe that one. How could something so terrifying turn out to be fun? But then, she supposed most of the older kids did laugh and mess around as they did their crazy dives. And when they came out of the water again, they were usually smiling like Adam had been that morning.

"I can help you during free swim if you want," Alex suggested. "Tyler said my dive was the straightest in the group."

The Tater Tot Jenna was munching on turned to dust in her mouth. Alex wasn't trying to make her feel better, she was just trying to show off. It was one more way for Alex to prove she was the better camper. She was about to tell Alex that she could handle her own diving when Marissa got up from the other end of the table, leaving the magazine with the other campers. She walked over and dropped down into the chair next to Jenna's.

"You guys were in such an intense conversation, I just *had* to see what was up," Marissa said, looking from Jenna to Alex. "So what's up?"

"I was just offering to help Jenna with her diving," Alex said.

"Oh, yeah. I heard about what happened this morning," Marissa said, looking at Jenna like she felt *so* bad for her.

It was all Jenna could do to keep from crawling under the table. "How did you hear about it?"

"Pete told me," Marissa said.

Jenna's jaw dropped. It wasn't surprising that Marissa had heard gossip from Pete. The two of them had been hanging out a lot this summer, and everyone suspected they might be dating. But she couldn't believe *Pete* had found out about it.

"How did Pete know?" Alex asked defensively, getting Jenna's back.

"I think Tyler told him," Marissa replied.

"Omigosh!" Jenna said, holding her head in her hand. "Everyone's talking about what a huge loser I am!"

"No! Jenna! It's not like that," Marissa said, putting her hand on Jenna's back. "I think Tyler was just asking for Pete's advice on how to help you."

"Great. So that just means that I'm so bad, even the swim instructor doesn't know what to do with me," Jenna said, slumping.

"Wow. Since when did you become so negative?"

Marissa asked.

Since now, Jenna thought. *Or maybe it started before I left home to come here.* It had been pretty tough to stay positive for those last few weeks of the school year. Normally Jenna looked forward to camp even more than she looked forward to Christmas, but this year everything had been different. Even leaving for camp wasn't as fun as it normally was.

"Want to hear a secret?" Marissa whispered.

Both Jenna and Alex perked up. There was nothing better than a secret. They all leaned closer to the table.

"I was afraid to dive until I was thirteen," Marissa told them.

Jenna and Alex glanced at each other, disbelieving.

"No way," Alex said.

"Way," Marissa said. "I was so pathetic. I was light-years behind my friends."

"So what finally made you do it?" Jenna asked, eyes wide.

"Well, I was standing with the younger campers on the beginners' pier, still petrified to dive, when I saw Marcy Brachfeld flirting with Tommy Catherwood by the diving boards," Marissa said. "I had a huge crush on Tommy, and there was no way I was letting Marcy have him, so I closed my eyes and dove off. Two days later Tommy was flirting with *me* by the diving boards," she added with a casual shrug.

Jenna and Alex giggled uncontrollably. "Okay, but I don't have a crush on anyone, so that's not going to make me dive," Jenna said finally.

"All I'm saying is, you never know what's going to

get you over that hurdle," Marissa told her. "But I think that having Alex help you during free swim is a great idea. It'll be much less pressure than trying to do it with all the yellows watching. And I'll be there, too, if you want. As a former non-diver, I should support you."

"Yeah?" Jenna said, glancing from Alex to Marissa. Everyone in the bunk loved Marissa, and the idea of getting the CIT all to herself made Jenna smile. Well, not *all* to herself, since Alex would be there. But Marissa wanted to take time out to hang with Jenna. And that was pretty cool.

"Yeah," Marissa said. "But Jenna, you've got to want to learn, or you'll never be able to do it."

"I know," Jenna said halfheartedly.

"That doesn't sound like someone who wants it," Marissa said.

That's because I'm still scared out of my mind, Jenna thought. "I do," she managed to say. "I want to learn how to dive." *But only so Chelsea can't pick on me, and I won't be compared to Adam or get left behind next year.*

"Good," Marissa said, patting her on the back.

"Good," Alex repeated with a confident nod.

"Good," Jenna said, trying to smile. But she shuddered when she thought of the lake looming below her. Jenna would never admit it in a million years, but suddenly she wished her mom and dad were there.

chapter

FOUR

"Jenna, you are a genius! Have I ever told you that you are a genius?" Grace whisper-giggled that evening.

"I know. I know. It's a gift, really," Jenna said with a shrug.

Jenna, Grace, and Alex were alone in the cabin with Marissa, who had turned on her Walkman and told them to pretend she wasn't there. Marissa knew what they were doing and, as a long camp legacy herself, had no problem with initiation pranks, as long as they were harmless. And of course, Jenna's initiation prank was always harmless.

Plus, it was fun. Messing around with Alex and Grace was even helping her forget about her awful afternoon. She, Alex, and Marissa had spent an hour on the pier, and Jenna hadn't done one dive. They were going to help her again tomorrow, but just thinking about it made Jenna ill. So she wasn't going to think about it.

"Here, put this in Chelsea's cubby," Alex said, handing Alyssa's art supplies to Grace. "Jenna, give me Chelsea's diary and I'll put it in Alyssa's cubby."

"Here. Hide it good and deep," Jenna said, handing over the glitter-covered book. She was still irritated with Chelsea for picking on her that morning at the lake. After that, Jenna was happier than ever that Alex had reminded her to pull the initiation prank. Chelsea so deserved it. "And let's put Natalie's makeup in Alyssa's, too," she added. "Oh, and give me that mix CD Alyssa's always listening to. We'll put it in Nat's."

"I mean, the way you got them out of the cabin!" Grace said, still giggling. "Telling them about the guys' nightly Wiffle ball game? That was perfect!"

"Yeah, especially for the guy crazies like Nat and Chelsea," Alex added, rolling her eyes. "I bet they're over there right now cheering on their favorite guys."

"Blech!" all three of them said in unison, sticking out their tongues.

"Yeah, but I thought Alyssa was never going to leave," Alex said, tossing Chelsea's favorite sandals into Natalie's cubby. "Brynn saved the day there."

"Totally," Jenna agreed.

At the last minute, when Alyssa had insisted for the tenth time that she did not have any interest in watching the guys play Wiffle ball, Brynn had stepped in and told her it would be a great story for the paper. The rivalry between Adam's bunk, 3F, and bunk 3E was almost as big as the one between Jenna's bunk and 3A. Tonight, 3F and 3E were playing each other during their free period, and Brynn had told Alyssa that she *had* to cover the game. Alyssa had finally, grudgingly, agreed and taken off with her pad and pencil. Jenna would really have to thank Brynn later.

Satisfied that they had switched up enough of the

newbies' stuff to be confusing, Jenna slapped her hands together and turned around. Now for the best part: the beds.

"You guys do Natalie and Chelsea," Jenna said. "I'll get Alyssa's. The top bunks are always harder."

"This is going to be so great!" Grace said as she tore the sheets off Natalie's bed. "I can't wait to see their faces."

Jenna grinned. For the first time all day she was in a perfectly giddy mood, and there wasn't a thought of diving or siblings or anything else in her mind. There was nothing like a good prank to cheer her up.

▲ ▲ ▲

That night, Jenna's heart pounded as she crawled into bed early and stayed near the edge, all the better to see the action. No one had noticed anything before dinner, and right after eating they had all gone to Classic Game Night in the main cabin. Sitting through several rounds of Coke and Pepsi, playing Red Rover with the guys, and watching the first-years go nuts during the Duck, Duck, Goose tournament had seemed to take forever. All Jenna wanted to do was see how Alyssa, Natalie, and Chelsea reacted to their initiation. Now, it was showtime.

Jenna caught Alex's eye as Chelsea went over to her cubby. She had to slap her hand over her mouth to hide her smile as Chelsea dug through the stuff that clearly wasn't hers. "Hey! Has anyone seen my diary?" Chelsea asked.

"No," Natalie said, pulling a few things out of her own cubby. "Have you seen my monogram pajamas?"

"Why would I have seen those?" Chelsea asked as Alyssa stepped up behind her.

"Oh, I don't know. Maybe because you have my paint set in your cubby," Alyssa said, whipping the tin out and holding it up. "What are you doing with this?"

Jenna buried her face in her pillow to keep from laughing. She could hear Grace and Brynn in the bathroom, wheezing for breath as they listened in.

"I didn't take your paints," Chelsea replied. "You must have put them in the wrong cubby."

"Wait a minute. Whose is this?" Natalie asked, pulling a black T-shirt out of her own cubby and holding it up between two fingers.

"That's mine, too!" Alyssa exclaimed, grabbing it away. "What's going on around here?"

Chelsea stalked over to Alyssa's cubby, pushed some things aside, and pulled out her diary. "Oh! And you accused *me*!" she shouted at Alyssa. "Who said you could read my private thoughts?"

"Trust me, I didn't even know you had thoughts," Alyssa said flatly.

Natalie cracked up laughing, but Chelsea just blinked as the joke went over her head. Jenna pounded her fist into her bed, practically crying, she was laughing so hard.

Then Chelsea finally got the insult and started shouting at Alyssa, who shouted right back. Natalie jumped between them, trying to calm them down, but it soon grew into a three-way fight.

"All right! All right! What's going on in here!?" Julie said, storming in from the porch, where she had been talking to another counselor.

Natalie, Alyssa, and Chelsea tried to explain all at once, and Julie's face gradually broke into a smile. She glanced from Jenna to Alex to Brynn and Grace, who were now standing in the bathroom doorway. All of them shrugged innocently.

"I don't know what's so funny!" Chelsea said to Julie. "Alyssa's a thief!"

"Girls! Girls! Calm down!" Julie finally said, holding up her hands. "I think you've officially been initiated."

"Welcome to bunk 3C!" Jenna and the other girls shouted, gathering around the newbies, cheering and clapping.

Natalie and the others looked stunned. "What?"

"Sorry, Nat," Jenna said, looping her arm around her friend's shoulder. "It had to be done."

"She's done it to all of us," Val explained.

"Except for the ones who started with us the first year," Alex explained.

"You're one of us now!" Grace shouted, hugging all three of the newbies in turn. "Congrats!"

Finally, Natalie, Alyssa, and Chelsea all seemed to get what was going on and started to smile.

"Omigod! I was ready to kill Alyssa for taking my diary," Chelsea said, covering her mouth.

"Not before I killed you for taking my paints," Alyssa replied, laughing as well.

"I *still* don't know where my pajamas are!" Natalie mock-whined.

"Here!" Jenna shouted, pulling them from the back of Alyssa's cubby and tossing them to Natalie.

"All right! Now let's everyone get to bed!" Julie

announced. "The fun's over, and it's time for lights-out. You can sort your stuff out in the morning."

Everyone groaned, and Natalie, Chelsea, and Alyssa quickly changed into their pajamas. Jenna and the other veteran campers climbed into bed and waited. Julie only *thought* the fun was over.

Natalie pulled back her blanket. Alyssa climbed to her top bunk. Chelsea fluffed her pillow. And then they all shoved their feet in under their sheets.

"Hey!" Chelsea exclaimed.

"What the . . . ?" Alyssa said.

"You *guys!*" Natalie wailed.

"Short-sheeting!" Jenna, Alex, Brynn, and Grace shouted, tossing their pillows toward the new girls.

And then, no matter how much Julie protested, the pillow fight of the century was launched.

▲ ▲ ▲

"Okay, Jenna, what scares you the most about diving?" Marissa asked as she, Jenna, and Alex stood on the edge of the beginner's pier again the following afternoon.

"Everything," Jenna replied.

"It can't be *everything*," Alex said, crossing her arms over her chest.

"Okay, fine. I just don't get how you're supposed to go headfirst," Jenna said, gesturing toward the water. "The water is so far down. And doesn't it hurt?"

"It doesn't, I promise," Alex said. "You just need to do it."

Jenna was starting to get tense with Alex breathing down her neck. It seemed like her idea of helping Jenna was standing there telling her to just do it. She was like a walking, talking Nike ad. It was a good thing Marissa had offered to help. If the CIT hadn't been there, Jenna probably would have given up by now.

"Okay, how about this?" Marissa said. "Why don't you try jumping into the water feetfirst? You can do that, right?"

"Everyone can do that," Jenna said with a scoff, stepping to the edge.

Marissa reached out and touched her arm before she could jump. "But this time, I want you to pay attention to your feet. Really think about how your feet feel when they hit the water, okay?"

Jenna blinked. Think about her feet? Was Marissa losing it? "Um . . . okay," she said.

She jumped off the platform, closed her eyes, and concentrated on her feet. They hit the water, Jenna felt the splash, and then went under. The water rushed up around her, refreshing and cool. Jenna smiled as she swam back up to the surface. She really did love to swim. If only she could just avoid the diving.

"Well?" Marissa asked.

"Well what?" Jenna replied, paddling over to the ladder.

"Did it hurt? Did your feet hurt when they hit the water?" Marissa asked.

Jenna paused as she climbed, thinking about it. "No."

"So if it doesn't hurt your feet when they go in first, it's not going to hurt your head, especially when your hands are breaking the water first," Marissa said happily.

"Wow. She's good," Alex said.

Jenna couldn't have agreed more. Marissa definitely had a point. Why would diving hurt any more than jumping?

"Okay, but what if I hit a rock?" Jenna asked, pulling her wet bathing suit away from her stomach to make the sucking sound she loved and then letting it go.

"Did you even hit the bottom of the lake when you jumped in just now?" Marissa asked.

Jenna felt her face flush slightly. "Um . . . no."

"Well then you're not going to hit it when you dive," Marissa told her. "Besides, there are no rocks down there. It's all sand."

"Swear?" Jenna asked.

"Cross my heart and hope to never wear eyeliner again," Marissa said. She crossed her heart with her finger and held up a flat hand like a Girl Scout.

"And for her, that's serious," Alex said.

Marissa and Jenna laughed, and Jenna walked to the edge of the platform once more, looking down. Suddenly, the water didn't seem as far away. Her stomach was still full of nervous butterflies, but for the first time, she felt like she might actually be able to do this. Marissa had done it when she was scared. Even Alex had told her that she had been a little frightened on her first dive. If they could both do it, why couldn't she?

Jenna turned to Marissa and Alex with a smile. "Okay! I think I'm gonna—"

"Hey, Marissa!"

Jenna's face fell when she saw her sister Stephanie walking the planks toward them. She was wearing her new pink tankini and her hair was back in a perfect

French braid.

"Hold that thought, J," Marissa said.

"What are you guys doing out here?" Stephanie asked, slipping on her Hollywood-style tinted sunglasses.

"We're helping Jenna with her diving," Alex announced.

Stephanie looked at Jenna sympathetically. "Oh, yeah, I heard about that, Boo." She stepped over and gathered Jenna's hair behind her head, running her fingers through it like Jenna's mother always did when Jenna was sad. Who did Stephanie think she was, Jenna's personal babysitter? This whole mothering thing was worse than ever this summer. "Anything I can do?" Stephanie asked. She stuck out her bottom lip slightly like she was talking to a pouting baby.

"Yeah. Stop calling me Boo," Jenna replied, stepping out of her sister's grasp.

"Oh, right! Sorry!" Stephanie said with a quick smile. She didn't actually seem sorry at all. "Listen, can I borrow Marissa for a sec? It's kind of important."

"Sure," Jenna said, mostly because Stephanie was already dragging Marissa aside.

"So, we *need* to talk about the social," Stephanie said.

"I know!" Marissa said. "We have to decide on wardrobe, makeup, and, most importantly—"

"Guys!" Marissa and Stephanie said at the same time, then giggled like a couple of crazy people.

Jenna and Alex looked at each other and rolled their eyes. It seemed like all the older girls talked about was which boys they liked and which boys liked them. Didn't they know there were about a million more important things in life? Like the fact that five seconds ago, Jenna had been ready to announce that she was going to take her first dive. Marissa was helping her with the most embarrassing problem of her life, and Stephanie had stolen her away. To talk about what? Stupid boys!

I'm never going to be able to dive now, Jenna thought, staring down at the water sadly. The moment of confidence had passed. She was back to being petrified. What had she been thinking?

"Hey! Here come the newbies," Alex said.

Natalie and Chelsea jogged toward the pier, both practically bursting, they were so excited.

"Omigod, you guys! You are never going to believe what just happened!" Natalie said, grabbing Jenna's arm. "Simon asked me to the social!"

"And Eric asked *me*!" Chelsea exclaimed.

Jenna's and Alex's jaw dropped. "What?" they both said in unison.

"I can't believe it! We have dates for the social!" Natalie trilled, grinning.

"Why?" Jenna asked. It was the only word in her head. "I mean . . . why?"

"What do you mean, why?" Chelsea asked with that superior look on her face. "It's a dance. You *have* to have a date for a dance or it's no fun."

"Uh, none of us has ever gone with dates before, and we always have fun," Alex said.

"Well, maybe things are going to be different this year," Chelsea replied.

Jenna could not believe it. Dates for the social? What was wrong with these girls? Why would they ever want to spend time with boys voluntarily? Jenna was forced to spend time with her brother and his friends all the time and it was just plain annoying. Plus, they were newbies and they were acting like the social was *their* thing. Like *they* knew how to make it fun. They had never even been to one before!

"Here they come!" Natalie whispered. "Act cool."

"Great. And your uglier half is with them," Alex joked.

Ugh! Could things get any worse? Adam, Simon, and Eric were all walking toward them, and Adam had that look on his face. That self-satisfied look he always got when he was feeling proud of himself about something. What had he done now, dove off the high dive?

Nat and Chelsea walked up to meet the boys and stopped a few feet up the pier. Alex shrugged and joined them while Adam stepped up to Jenna at the edge of the planks.

"Hey, Jen," Adam said. "Why so bummed? No date for the dance?"

"Like I want one," Jenna said. "Wait. Don't tell me *you* have one."

"Uh . . . no. No ball and chain for me," Adam joked. "So if it's not a guy, then what's with the face? You're all scrunchy."

"I don't know, it's like all anyone can talk about is the social. Like it's *so* important. Look at Stephanie," Jenna grumbled, glaring at her sister and Marissa over her shoulder. "Marissa was helping me out, and Stephanie came over to discuss wardrobe and guys or whatever and now it's like I'm invisible."

"You could never be invisible!" Adam said. "Especially not in that bathing suit," he added with a laugh, eyeing her yellow and pink Hawaiian-print tank.

"Shut up!" Jenna shot back.

"Okay! Okay!" Adam said. "God! Freak out a little more, why don't you? What's the big deal?"

Jenna glanced at Stephanie and Marissa, laughing and whispering. The big deal was Marissa was supposed to be hanging out with *her*. But once again one of her siblings had to come along and ruin her afternoon for her. And now Adam was here to rub salt in the wound. "Just forget it," Jenna told Adam.

"Well, if you want help with your diving, I can help you," Adam offered.

Like I really want my twin brother coaching me. How humiliating, Jenna thought. "Thanks, anyway," she said.

"Come on, Jen, I'm already at *blue* level," Adam said. "I can help."

"Oh, you're so cool," Jenna said, annoyed. "You're already at blue level." *I would* kill *to be at blue level*, she added silently.

"I'm sorry I'm ahead of you, all right? But if you don't learn how to dive, you're going to be stuck back here in yellow while the rest of your friends move on to green and blue," Adam said.

Like I don't know this, Jenna thought, heat prickling at the back of her neck. Why couldn't everyone just leave her alone? Why did they have to keep reminding her of what a failure she was?

I want to call Mom, Jenna thought, then felt like a big baby. Her mother had plenty of other things to worry about this summer. She didn't need her daughter calling her up to whine about diving like she was some kindergartner.

"Come on. I'll practice with you," Adam said.

Why did everyone feel the need to push her? All it did was make her feel worse. Jenna had to get out of there before she did something embarrassing. Like burst into tears. Thinking about her mother had already made the hot prickling move into her eyes. The last thing she wanted to do was cry in front of everyone.

"Thanks, anyway, but I . . . uh . . . I kind of need to go to the bathroom right now," Jenna said, backing up. It was the first excuse that came to mind.

"Jenna—"

"Really, Adam," Jenna said, turning. She was so frustrated, and somehow, even with all these people around, she felt really alone. "I gotta go."

She turned and jogged to the beach, grabbing up her board shorts and flip-flops from the end of the pier. Jenna would have loved to have run back to the bunk and cry her eyes out, but she wasn't allowed to leave the lake area during free swim. Some of the girls from 3C were lounging over by the first-aid shack. Jessie and Grace both had their noses buried in books while Candace, Valerie, and Alyssa flipped through magazines. Everyone else was swimming in the shallow end, but she couldn't face her friends when she was all red-eyed and upset. Instead, she headed for a huge oak tree behind the water sports cabin, which also housed the bathrooms. She dropped to the ground in front of it, pulled her knees up under her chin and hugged them to her.

I am so sick of my brothers and sister, Jenna thought, burying her face behind her legs. *Next year I'm going to a different camp. Or better. I'll make Mom and Dad send all of them to a different camp.*

"Jenna? Are you okay?"

Sniffling quickly, Jenna was surprised to find Chelsea hovering over her. Had she actually left the precious boys to see if Jenna was all right?

"I'm fine," Jenna said grouchily.

Chelsea tucked her blond hair behind her ear and sat down next to Jenna. After two weeks at camp, Chelsea already had a deep tan, and the freckles across the bridge of her nose were more defined. She was wearing a baby blue bathing suit that brought out the stunning color of her eyes. In fact, Jenna now realized that all of Chelsea's bathing suits were blue, and for the first time she wondered if Chelsea had matched her eyes on purpose. Jenna looked down at her own bright suit. Matching her clothes to her eyes was something she never would have thought of doing. But that was Chelsea.

"Hey, I'm sorry I picked on you the other day," Chelsea said, putting her arm around Jenna. "I didn't know it was such a big deal."

"It's not," Jenna replied automatically.

"Okay," Chelsea said quickly.

They both stared at the ground for a moment. Jenna watched a trail of ants returning to their anthill in a perfect line.

"I am *so* glad I don't have a brother," Chelsea said finally.

"Adam is such a jerk," Jenna replied. " 'I'm in blue, you know.' Like we don't *all* know he's ahead of the rest of us."

"He's so obnoxious," Chelsea agreed. "We need to get back at him."

Jenna lifted her head fully for the first time. Chelsea's eyes gleamed with mischief. "Get back at him? How?"

"Nothing big," Chelsea said with a shrug. "Just a small, innocent prank—like the one you pulled on us last night. To remind him who he's dealing with."

Jenna smiled slightly. A prank. Yes. That would make her feel better. Pulling a prank always made her feel better. It would take her mind off diving, off Adam and Stephanie, off her parents. She grinned at Chelsea. Just yesterday Jenna had been beyond mad at the girl for picking on her fear of diving, but suddenly that didn't matter anymore. If there was one thing Chelsea would be good for, it was pranking. She was fearless and smart. And she didn't care what anyone else thought of her, which could be a pain sometimes, but it made her the perfect partner in crime. And that was exactly what Jenna needed at the moment.

"We need a plan," Jenna said. "A really, *really* good one."

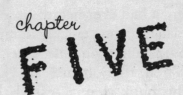

chapter
FIVE

Chelsea and Jenna stood in the bunk bathroom that evening, huddled in the corner by the second toilet. It had started to drizzle outside toward the end of free swim, and the light rain tapped against the windowpane above their heads. As always, the rain brought out the slight moldy smell of the bathroom and made the air thick. Out in the bunk, the rest of Jenna's friends killed the free time before dinner by writing letters to their parents and friends. Jenna, however, was doing what she did best: plotting.

"Are you sure you can do this?" she asked Chelsea under her breath. "I can, if you want me to. I can fake it better than anybody."

"Come on, Jenna. Julie's never going to believe you have a stomachache," Chelsea said. "You're you."

"Yeah. I guess I have used it too many times," Jenna said, checking her plastic watch. "Okay, we gotta do it now or we won't have time."

"Let's go," Chelsea said with a nod.

Jenna lifted a twenty-ounce bottle of Sunkist her dad had sent in a care package. She nodded at Chelsea, who coughed so that no one would hear the hiss as she popped the bottle open. Then Jenna nodded again, and Chelsea started making some of the most convincing barfing noises Jenna had ever heard.

Stifling a laugh, Jenna quickly dumped the Sunkist into the toilet so it would sound like Chelsea was actually throwing up. When they heard an "Ew" and some movement in the bunk, Jenna tossed the bottle into the trash and Chelsea hit her knees, quickly flushing the toilet. Seconds later Julie appeared in the doorway with half the bunk gathered behind her.

"Who's sick?" Julie asked, her eyes darting to Chelsea.

Chelsea took a deep, heaving breath. Her hair stuck to her forehead as she looked up at Julie with heavy eyes.

"I don't feel so good," Chelsea said.

"She threw up. A lot," Jenna confirmed, doing her best grossed-out face.

Julie crouched next to Chelsea and pushed her hair back from her face. Jenna was impressed to see Chelsea swallowing hard and hanging her head. The girl knew what she was doing. If Jenna didn't know better, even *she* would have believed Chelsea was ill. Suddenly Jenna had a whole new respect for this particular new girl.

"Can you make it to the nurse's cabin?" Julie asked.

"I don't know," Chelsea said weakly.

"I'll take her," Jenna volunteered. As if the idea had just come to her.

Julie helped Chelsea to her feet, where she stood, leaning sideways slightly like she was about to fall over.

"Chelsea? Do you need me to go with you, or is

Jenna okay?" Julie asked.

"No. Jenna's fine," Chelsea said, adding a burp. "You have to take everyone to dinner." She put her hand over her stomach and grimaced. "Ugh. Dinner."

"I'd better get her out of here before she ralphs again," Jenna said, wrapping her arm around Chelsea. Together they staggered to the bathroom door, where everyone parted to let them through.

"Here, you guys," Grace said, helpfully grabbing their windbreakers from the pegs by the door. "It's raining out, and you don't want Chelsea to get even sicker."

"Yeah, you don't want her to get even sicker," Candace repeated.

"Thanks," Jenna said, feeling a little guilty over Grace's concern and thoughtfulness. She and Chelsea struggled into their jackets and headed out into the drizzle.

"Feel better!" Val called after them.

Then the screen door slammed shut, and Jenna and Chelsea made their way around the bunk. As soon as they were safely out of sight, Jenna stopped pretending to hold Chelsea up and they took off at a run, heading for the mess hall. The plan was simple, but it had to be done within the next five minutes, or they were sure to get caught.

Jenna's heart pounded as her feet slammed along the muddy path through the woods. She loved this energized feeling she got whenever she was about to pull a prank. She was half-psyched, half-nervous, but couldn't stop grinning. When Jenna was pulling a prank it was like the rest of the world and all its problems melted away. All that was left was fun.

Chelsea emerged into the clearing behind the

mess hall first. Jenna looked both ways. The coast was clear. They sprinted to the back of the building and leaned against the wooden planked wall.

"Whew. Made it," Chelsea said, wiping some rain off her cheek.

"I'll peek inside," Jenna offered.

As always, the back door to the kitchen was open to let the air in while the cooks slaved over the hot stoves. Ever so slowly Jenna checked around the side of the door. The three cooks and Pete were all standing at the huge silver stoves, talking and laughing as they stirred huge vats of torture food.

Ugh. Smells like beef Stroganoff, Jenna thought, scrunching up her nose. This would be one of those bread-only nights for her, but it was good news for the prank. Her brother *loved* that gooey brown mess.

"Jenna! Come on!" Chelsea whispered.

Pulse pounding in her ears, Jenna reached up to the shelf next to the door and grabbed down a five-pound bag of sugar. She was pressed back into the outside wall again before anyone was the wiser.

"It's so great how they keep all this stuff right by the door," Jenna said, hugging the bag to her. "It's like they're *asking* us to steal it."

"Okay, let's go," Chelsea said.

Crouching low below the windows, Jenna and Chelsea made their way around the side of the mess hall to the front. Mud splattered Jenna's sneakers, and rain dripped from her hood onto her nose. When they reached the door, Chelsea peeked inside and quickly jumped back. "The CITs are still setting the tables," she informed Jenna.

"Count to ten and check again," Jenna said.

Together, they counted up to ten Mississippis, then Chelsea checked.

"Okay! They're all back in the kitchen. It's now or never," Chelsea said.

They locked eyes, filled with excitement, then Jenna nodded. "Go!"

Jenna and Chelsea ran into the mess hall, right over to Adam's table. There were three sets of plastic salt and pepper shakers, and Jenna grabbed them all up while Chelsea slid under the table. Jenna joined her and opened the salt bottles while Chelsea ripped open the bag of sugar. They sat, cross-legged and facing each other. That was when Jenna noticed a snag in the plan.

"What do I do with the salt?" Jenna whispered, her heart pounding wildly.

"Oh, God! Why didn't we think of that?" Chelsea asked.

Jenna looked around and was hit with an idea. "My pockets!"

"Nice!" Chelsea replied.

Jenna quickly emptied all three salt shakers into her jacket pockets. Chelsea grabbed the bottles one by one and dipped them into the sugar bag to fill them.

"This is gonna be so great," Chelsea said with a snicker.

"I know!" Jenna whispered back.

Just as Jenna was replacing all the shaker tops, they heard the door from the kitchen bang open.

Jenna froze, a chill of fear sliding over her from head to toe. Chelsea grabbed her hand. Their palms were both covered in sweat—or maybe it was just rain.

Either way, Jenna could practically hear her friend's heart beating.

"You were supposed to make sure all the glasses from lunch got cleaned!" someone scolded. "What are we supposed to do with ten dozen dirty glasses?"

"Whatever. It's too late to do anything now. Don't say anything and no one will notice," another voice answered.

Jenna and Chelsea both stuck out their tongues. So much for drinking any bug juice tonight. The two sets of feet clomped right by their table and out the front door.

"That was close," Chelsea said.

Jenna nodded her agreement. "Let's get out of here."

They checked first to make sure the coast was clear, then quickly replaced all the salt and pepper shakers on Adam's table. It was all Jenna could do to keep from laughing out loud as they raced out the front door and turned their steps toward the nurse's cabin.

"Omigosh! This is going to be so funny!" Chelsea cried, dumping the rest of the sugar in the nearest garbage can.

Jenna shook the salt out of her pockets and it rained down, disappearing into the grass. "I know! Beef Stroganoff is bad enough, but beef Stroganoff with sugar? Gag me!"

"Come on! We have to get to the nurse's station and tell her I was sick but that the fresh air cured me," Chelsea said. "There's no way I'm missing this!"

They grabbed hands and ran for the nurse's station to cover their tracks in case Julie followed up with Nurse Helen later. Jenna could barely wait to get to dinner. So much for Adam thinking she couldn't pull a prank on him. He had no idea what was about to hit him!

▲ ▲ ▲

The key to getting away with a prank was to keep from laughing before everyone else did. Only the prankster herself would know to laugh *before* anything happened. Jenna had learned this when she had planted her first whoopee cushion on her teacher's chair, then cracked up before his butt hit the seat. He had stopped, found the cushion, and sent her directly to the principal's office. But even though she knew this very important rule, Jenna was having a very hard time keeping a straight face while Adam and his friends covered their dinner in sugar.

"I can't take it," Chelsea whispered in her ear. There was a laugh right on the edge of her voice. "I really can't take it."

"When are they going to eat it already?" Jenna replied.

"Are you okay down there, Chelsea?" Julie asked from the head of the table. "Only eat the bland stuff."

"Oh, I am," Chelsea replied, tearing off a piece of her white bread for good measure. Neither she nor Jenna had touched their drinks *or* their dinners. Later, after lights-out, they planned on raiding Jenna's candy stash to keep away the hungries until morning.

"Here we go," Jenna said into her napkin.

She and Chelsea stared as Adam, his friend Eric, and his counselor Nate all took their first bites of food. Adam's eyes bulged. Then he gagged. Then Eric knocked over Adam's bug juice while grabbing for his own, splashing the yellow liquid all over Adam.

"Hey!" Adam shouted, jumping up.

At that point, Jenna and Chelsea couldn't take it anymore. They cracked up laughing. Luckily, half the kids at Adam's table and the rest of the kids at neighboring tables were laughing, too. Spilled bug juice always got a big reaction.

Adam, meanwhile, seemed to forget his wet lap and remembered the taste in his mouth. He stuck his tongue out a few times like a frog and grabbed Eric's glass right out of his hands, chugging down half the bug juice.

Jenna nearly doubled over, she was laughing so hard. Chelsea had tears coming out of her eyes.

Before they realized what was going on, a couple of the other guys took huge mouthfuls of food. One of them grabbed his napkin and spit the beef into it. Another just spit it right back onto his plate.

"Ew!" Grace squealed.

"Ew!" Candace echoed.

"Pete! What's with the Stroge?" Nate called out. Nate had a habit of shortening any word with more than two syllables.

"Oh, that is so gross," Brynn put in as another of the boys tasted his dinner, then spit it out half-chewed.

Pete walked over to the table. "Problem, man?" he asked Nate. "Did you salt it? You know you always gotta salt the Stroge."

Jenna and Chelsea laughed even harder. This was too perfect for words.

"Of course we salted it," Nate said.

Pete shrugged and bravely grabbed a fork to take

a bite of Nate's food. His lips pursed, but he somehow managed to swallow. "Dude. That beef is covered in sugar," he said.

"Sugar?" Nate replied. He grabbed a shaker and shook some sugar into his palm, then tasted it. "I don't believe it."

Adam and Simon tested the other shakers. "They're all full of sugar," Simon announced.

"Oh, gross! Sugar on beef?" Alex said, sticking out her tongue. "Who would do *that*?"

Instantly everyone at the surrounding tables looked over at Jenna. Jenna and Chelsea stared back, their eyes wide with innocence.

"Jenna? Chelsea? Did you really go to the nurse's before dinner?" Julie asked, sounding weary.

"What? Julie! I was barfing. Of course we did," Chelsea said.

Julie narrowed her blue eyes. "You *have* made a stunning recovery."

"Nurse Helen said her lunch just didn't agree with her," Jenna told Julie. "You can ask her yourself."

"I think I will," Julie said as Pete and Nate started clearing away all the plates of food from Adam's table. "And, Chelsea, don't take this the wrong way, but I hope, for your sake, that you actually were sick."

chapter SIX

"So, you guys did it, right? I mean, you have to have done it," Grace said, her eyes shining with excitement as she questioned Jenna a few days later. They were at their photography elective and since it was raining again, they were inside, working on printing the nature photos they had taken earlier in the week.

"Grace! Adam is *right there!*" Jenna said through her teeth. She was trying to feed the film through the negative carrier doohickey, and she kept getting it jammed. This photography thing wasn't as easy at it looked.

"So you did! I knew it!" Grace said with a grin. The rain had made Grace's curly hair frizz out, so she had tied it into two short braids. The hairdo and her excited face both made her seem about four years younger than she was.

Jenna glanced at her brother over her shoulder. Everyone she knew had been asking her the same question ever since beef Stroganoff night, but Jenna always denied it. The last thing she needed was for Julie to find out and punish her somehow, or for Adam to find out and fight back. But she was dying to tell someone that she had pulled it off. What good was pulling a prank if you couldn't take credit for your creativity? Luckily Adam was busy studying his film strips. He seemed to be taking this whole photography thing very seriously.

"Come on, Jenna. Tell me," Grace said. "I'm dying over here."

"Okay, yeah, we did," Jenna said with a sly grin.

Grace squealed in delight and slapped her hand over her mouth.

"But don't tell anyone!" Jenna added. "Nurse Helen backed up our story, but if Julie finds out, she's going to murder us."

"I'll never tell. Even if they torture me," Grace said with a grin. She kept giggling as she sorted through her film negatives, and Jenna knew that Grace was happy to be the only one let in on the prank. "Chelsea totally tricked me. I thought she was really sick."

"Yeah. Sorry about that," Jenna said, her guilt from the other day returning. "I felt bad for making everyone worry."

"Eh. It was Chelsea. We weren't *that* worried," Grace joked. Then her face fell. "Oh! That was mean! I was just kidding!"

"I know! I know!"

Jenna laughed and finally managed to get the film strip straight in the negative carrier, which was a flat plate with a slot in the middle.

"Grace? Can you read me the next step?" Jenna said over her shoulder.

Faith had given them all a list of the steps for printing photographs, and Grace had one on the table in front of her.

Grace looked down at the paper and shrugged. "Here," she said, handing the list to Jenna. "I . . . I don't know how much you've already done."

"Oookay," Jenna said, taking the page from Grace. She read the directions quickly and found the next step: *Insert negative carrier into enlarger.*

The enlarger looked kind of like a projector. She put the carrier into the machine. Then she turned on the light, and her picture appeared on the empty tray below.

"Wow! It actually works!" Jenna said.

Her picture was of a squirrel holding an acorn. She could see the image projected onto the tray in front of her. Jenna was sure that Faith, the photography instructor, had explained the science behind the whole process, but Jenna had zoned out during that part, replaying in her mind the scene of Adam choking on his beef Stroganoff.

She had been replaying the scene a lot over the last few days, actually. It was just so perfect!

Jenna focused her image so it would print as sharply as possible. Then she switched off the light so she could insert the photographic paper into the tray without exposing it. Once it was ready, she flipped on the light that was going to magically affix her picture to the paper. She sat back to wait. In her mind she saw Adam, hands grabbing for his throat in slow motion as he tasted his beef-with-sugar. She saw him gagging, saw Eric knocking over the bug juice, saw the splash and Adam's surprised face. Jenna only wished she could have videotaped the whole thing to show over and over and over . . .

"Jenna! What're you doing!?"

Startled out of her daydream, Jenna stood up to find Adam glaring at her. Oh, no! Had she zoned out so far, she had actually confessed to the crime or something?

"Your paper's not straight! Your picture's gonna be all crooked," Adam said, gesturing at her enlarger.

"Geez! Sorry, Mr. Perfect."

She undid the little flaps that held the paper in place and adjusted it.

"No! You can't move it once the light's already on!" Adam said, his eyes wide.

"Oh, right," Jenna said, remembering the instructions. Her face flushed, and she resecured the paper, but it was too late now. She had already moved it. What was going to happen to her photo?

"And how long has the light been on, anyway? Did you even set the timer?" Adam asked.

"The timer!" Jenna exclaimed. She had been so focused on daydreaming about her prank, she had missed the most basic step. She reached over and turned the light off, and Adam shook his head like he just couldn't believe how stupid she was.

"What?" Jenna said, pulling her photo paper out of the tray. "I'm sure it's going to come out fine."

Trying to look more confident than she felt, Jenna walked over to the tubs of chemicals near the wall and slid her photo into the developing liquid. Much to her disappointment, Adam followed as if he was determined to see if she had messed up. Jenna snapped on a pair of plastic gloves and waited.

See? I remembered the gloves. I know what I'm doing, Jenna thought. *I paid attention!*

Grace joined Adam and Jenna at the developer and they all leaned in to watch as the image appeared. This was the best part, as far as Jenna was concerned. Watching

Faith's photos magically appear during her demonstration had been totally cool.

"Which picture did you choose, Jenna?" Faith asked, joining them. Her small glasses were perched at the end of her nose, and her long brown hair was pulled back in a low ponytail. She wasn't much older than Julie and the other counselors, but she tried to make herself look like she was.

"It's a picture of a squirrel holding an acorn," Jenna said proudly. "I think it's really good."

That moment something started to appear on the page, but it didn't look anything like a squirrel. At first, there was a big black blob right in the middle, surrounded by other fuzzy blobs that could only be the leaves and rocks the squirrel had been sitting on. Behind the center blob, there were a bunch of gray speckles. Then the image started to turn darker and darker.

Pressing her lips together, Jenna grabbed the photo out of the developer and put it into the stop bath, which was what they called the liquid in the next bin. At least she remembered that part.

"Oh, Jenna," Faith said. "It's okay. The great thing about having a negative is that you can try to print from it again and again until it comes out the way you want it."

"And you definitely didn't want it *that* way," Adam said.

"Don't listen to him," Grace said. "Your next one will be fabulous. I know it," she added, looping her arm around Jenna and sticking her tongue out at Adam.

Jenna couldn't have been more grateful for Grace's save, because she never could have said anything herself. She knew that if she opened her mouth, she was going to burst into tears. She stared down at her blackened photo, her face burning with embarrassment. For a veteran Lakeview camper who thought she knew how to do everything, Jenna was certainly getting a lot wrong lately. And she didn't like the way it felt.

▲ ▲ ▲

By that afternoon the rain had stopped, though the sky remained overcast. It was a little windy and chilly, but as long as there was no water falling from the sky, free swim was still on. As the rest of the campers streamed from their bunks, laughing and screeching, their towels billowing behind them as they ran for the lake, Jenna trudged behind her friends. It used to be that free swim was Jenna's favorite part of the day. Now she was just wishing the rain would come back so they could all hang out in the cabin and play cat's cradle and checkers and Clue. Jenna was starting to hate the lake.

"Cheer up, Jenna," Julie said, falling into step with her. "If the weather keeps up like this, at least we'll still get to have the scavenger hunt tonight."

Jenna brightened a bit as Julie quickened her steps to catch up with Marissa at the head of the crowd. Scavenger hunts were the best evening activity there was. And since Jenna knew the camp like the back of her hand, her group always completed their lists and brought home the blue ribbon.

"What's a scavenger hunt?" Natalie asked as she and Valerie caught up with Jenna.

"What's a scavenger hunt?" Jenna repeated, her jaw dropping. "You've never done one?"

"Um . . . no," Natalie said. "Doesn't sound like a New York kind of event."

"Omigosh, scavenger hunts are the best," Jenna said, warming to the topic. She loved being able to teach the newbies like Natalie about camp traditions. "You get this whole long list of things that you have to find, and whoever finds the most stuff on their list, wins."

"What kind of things?" Natalie asked, interested.

"Everything from a single acorn to a four-leaf clover to a napkin from the mess hall, or one of Pete's baseball caps," Jenna said. "It's different every year."

"Yeah, but last year we were the only ones to get one of Pete's caps," Grace added, joining the group. "Thanks to Jenna."

"You stole one of his caps?" Natalie asked.

"I would have, but he found out that they were on the list, so he hid them all," Jenna replied. "Not even his own bunk could find them."

"So how did you get one?" Natalie asked.

"She talked him into giving her one," Valerie replied, hooking her arm around Jenna. "The girl is good."

Jenna grinned as everyone agreed. It was the baseball cap that had helped them beat out bunk 4A last year and take first place.

"So? How did you talk him into it?" Natalie asked.

"Well, last year my big brother Matt was still a counselor here and he had these two tickets to that AlternaFest concert at the end of the summer," Jenna said. "Everyone knew he had them and that he hadn't decided who to bring yet, so I just told Pete that if he gave me the cap, I'd tell Matt how he had helped me out. Then Matt would think he was really cool and take him to the concert. After that, he finally gave in."

"Jenna? That's not talking him into it, that's bribery," Natalie said with a laugh.

"Whatever it was, it worked," Valerie said.

"So did Pete get to go to the concert?" Natalie asked.

"Nah," Jenna said. "Matt took his new girlfriend, Keira, but Pete said he understood because she was 'so totally hot,'" she added, doing her best Pete impression.

Everyone laughed as they reached the lake. As Grace and Valerie dropped their stuff, a couple of guys from 3F walked over to them.

"Hey, Val. You swimming?" one of them asked.

Valerie flushed and smiled. "Yeah. I'll be right in."

"Cool," he said. Then he and his friends turned and ran for the water.

"Who was that?" Jenna asked.

"His name's Christopher. He's a newbie," Val said. "He asked me to the social this morning."

Jenna's heart dropped. *"You* have a date, too?"

Val shrugged, and Grace groaned. "Everyone is going to have a date except me!" Grace said.

"No way," Jenna said. "*I* am not going to have a date, and neither is Alex or Sarah or any of us who haven't gone totally boingo bonkers."

"Yeah, Grace," Natalie said. "Don't feel like you have to have a date or something. It's not a big deal."

"All right, but you have to swear that you will not have a date," Grace said to Jenna, her face more serious than Jenna had ever seen it. Apparently this whole date thing was really getting to her.

"I swear on my life I will not have a date," Jenna said.

Grace broke into a grin. "Thanks, Jenna. Come on, Val. Let's swim!"

Valerie and Grace raced to the water, but Jenna hung back. Natalie placed her bag on the ground and glanced at Jenna.

"You going in?" Natalie asked.

"I don't really feel like swimming," Jenna said. She wrapped her arms around herself, trying to look cold.

Natalie looked from her friends splashing in the water back to Jenna. "Do you want to practice diving? 'Cuz I could come with you."

Jenna instantly tensed. "That's okay."

"I learned how to dive when I was really young. My mom made me take lessons from the time I could, like, stand up," Natalie said. "It took me a while, too, but it's totally fun once you get into it. Maybe I could help."

"Why does everyone think I need help?" Jenna snapped, her good mood gone. Her arms dropped to her sides, and her fingers curled up into angry fists.

Natalie's face fell. "Well, I just—"

"I don't, okay? I don't need help from you or Adam or anyone," Jenna said. "I just don't feel like swimming."

With that, she placed her towel down on the grass and sat, her knees pulled up under her chin. Natalie hovered for a second, but Jenna just stared out at the gray sky and the even grayer water. She couldn't believe that Natalie, a first-year camper, was offering to help her out with something. Jenna was a total veteran compared to her. *She* was supposed to be helping *Natalie* with stuff. Not the other way around.

"All right," Natalie said with a shrug. "I'll be hanging out with Simon if you change your mind."

Jenna stayed angry for only a few seconds as she watched Natalie join the boys and saw the rest of her friends doing gymnastic moves in the water. Then she started to feel awful. Jenna had practically bitten Natalie's head off, and Natalie had still left the door open for Jenna to ask for help. Natalie was so friendly, and Jenna had just treated her like a jerk. What was wrong with her?

Normally, Jenna was pretty easygoing, but she just couldn't seem to take it anymore. She couldn't take everyone reminding her of what a loser she was. She had thought that coming to camp would help her get her mind off the things that were going on back home, but it was like the longer she stayed here, the worse she felt. And the worse she felt, the harder it was to keep from showing it. The first two weeks of camp had been okay, getting to know new people and getting back into the swing of things, but the more she settled into her routine, the harder it was to act like everything was okay. All she wanted to do was go back to last summer, when camp was still fun—back when she knew what she was doing.

chapter SEVEN

After half an hour of sitting by herself in the sand, Jenna got bored and asked Tyler for a special pass to go back to her bunk. She told him she didn't feel well, and all he had to do was take one look at her sad face and he believed her. Normally campers weren't allowed to wander off by themselves, but Tyler took pity on Jenna. He told her that since she knew the camp so well, being a fourth-year and all, he would let her go, but she had to keep to the path and go straight back. For once, Jenna had no problem following a rule. At that moment, all she wanted to do was lie down on her bunk and sulk.

But as she cut through the woods, Jenna started to feel a little better. Here she was, walking back to her bunk all by herself. Natalie never would have been allowed to do that. She wasn't experienced enough and didn't know her way around. There were still perks to being Jenna.

High above, the sun started to break through the clouds, causing the droplets of rain on the leaves to dance and sparkle. The birds in the trees woke up and started chirping as if it were morning and not late afternoon. Jenna passed by the rock where she, Alex, and Brynn used to hang out and trade gum when they were second-years. She saw the tree where Matt had carved his initials with the rest of his bunk. When she came to the edge of the clearing by the cabins, she saw the old, crumbling tool shed where she and her friends had hid last year after raiding the boys' cabin. This was Camp Lakeview, her home-away-from-home. It was impossible to stay depressed here for long.

Hey, maybe Marissa's hanging out in the cabin, Jenna realized suddenly, quickening her steps as she passed by the other bunks. Marissa and the other CITs usually got a break during free swim since they had to work meals and all other hours of the day. Hanging out with Marissa would cheer her up. Maybe Jenna could even get her to tell the story of her first dive again and try to get back some of that confidence.

Jenna bounded up the steps and yanked open the screen door, hoping to find Marissa on her cot, flipping through the latest copy of *Allure*. Instead, she found Marissa and Stephanie sitting cross-legged in the middle of the bunk floor, doing their nails. The whole bunk was filled with the sour scent of nail polish remover. Jenna stopped in her tracks.

"Hey! What are you doing here?" Marissa asked. Her tone was totally normal, but the question made Jenna feel like an outsider in her own bunk.

"I didn't feel well, so Tyler said I could come back," Jenna replied.

"What's wrong?" Stephanie asked, her face all-concern. "Is it your stomach? Your head?"

"Don't worry about it, *Mom*," Jenna said, instantly

grouchy again. "I just want to lie down." She so didn't want to be babied right now. Why did her sister have to be there? Couldn't Jenna ever get Marissa all to herself? Marissa was supposed to be Jenna's CIT. She was supposed to be here for *Jenna*, not Stephanie.

"Okay, but if you need anything, you just let me know," Stephanie said. "We Blooms have to take care of each other," she added with a wink.

Gag me, Jenna thought.

"You're lucky you have your sister at camp with you," Marissa told Jenna with a smile. "Especially since I never know what to do when campers are sick. I become Panic Girl. The not-so-super-hero," she joked.

"Yeah. So lucky," Jenna said flatly. "Nice polish, Marissa," she added, standing awkwardly off to the side. She wasn't sure whether she should join them or stick with her story and crawl into her bunk. Could she really just lie there while Marissa and Stephanie had fun without her?

"Thanks," Marissa said, snapping her gum as she held up her fingers to check them. "It's called Very Berry. Wanna try some?"

Jenna was about to say yes when Stephanie cut her off. "Oh, please. Polish is pointless on Jenna. She bites her nails to bits."

Flushing, Jenna hid her hands behind her back. Her nails *were* a little destroyed, but Stephanie didn't have to announce it like Jenna was some kind of joke.

"So, you're going to wear your red sundress?" Stephanie asked Marissa.

"I think so," Marissa replied. "And you have to wear that new mini. The boys will go speechless."

"You guys are talking about the social, aren't you?" Jenna asked, dropping onto Natalie's bottom bunk. *"Again."*

"Like there's anything else to talk about around here," Stephanie said with a laugh.

How about we talk about you getting out of my cabin? Jenna thought, though she knew she'd never say it.

"So, Jenna, what are you going to wear?" Stephanie asked. "I hope you brought something cool this year."

Jenna's expression darkened. Was Stephanie trying to say she had looked like a dork at every other camp dance? Jenna thought of the lavender dress with the lace on the sleeves that she had brought for this year's event. When she had packed it she'd thought it was perfect, but with Stephanie and Marissa talking about red dresses and denim minis, now it just seemed way too babyish.

"Who cares what I wear?" Jenna said. "It's just the stupid camp dance."

"Social," Marissa and Stephanie reminded her, then laughed as if there was some kind of personal joke between them.

"Whatever," Jenna said, finally giving up. She climbed up into her bunk and lay down on her side, on top of the covers. Staring at her colorful collection of bumper stickers that were taped to the wall, Jenna fumed over her sister. Who did she think she was, criticizing her clothes and trying to take care of her like a mother? And why did she have to hang around Jenna's bunk so much? Couldn't she just leave her alone?

Jenna sighed. She reached out and flattened the

bent corner on her Six Flags Great Adventure sticker.

I should prank her next, she thought as she listened to her sister and Marissa discussing all the CITs and counselors at camp, predicting who would kiss by the end of the summer and which couples would break up. Totally boring. *Oh, yeah, Stephanie is in total need of a pranking*, she thought. *If only because it'll give her something else to talk about!*

▲ ▲ ▲

"Where are they?" Jenna asked, bouncing up and down on the balls of her feet.

"I don't know, but I'm getting worried," Alex said. "3A just ran by, and they looked psyched."

"We cannot let 3A win," Brynn said. "We just can't."

It was the middle of the scavenger hunt, and Jenna and the rest of her bunk were waiting for Val, Sarah, and Grace to return from the sports shed. At Jenna's feet was a pillowcase full of items from the list. All they needed to complete it were a horseshoe, which Val and the others were getting, and the last bonus item, which even Jenna hadn't figured out how to get. Not yet, anyway.

"There they are!" Natalie cried, pointing toward the edge of the woods.

Sure enough, Valerie, Grace, and Sarah were all running toward them, red-faced and gasping for air.

"We got it! We got the last horseshoe!" Valerie whispered.

"Did 3A get one?" Chelsea demanded.

"Yeah," Sarah said, bending at the waist. "They got

there right before us."

"Now we *have* to get this last item to win," Jenna said, holding up the list. "But how are we supposed to get a picture of the top of a counselor's head?"

"What kind of scavenger hunt *is* this?" Alyssa asked.

"Yeah! What kind of scavenger hunt *is* this?" Candace echoed.

"An unfair one," Sarah said, gesturing at a couple of counselors as they walked by. "They all saw the list beforehand, so they're all wearing hats. We can't get a picture of the top of their heads if they won't take their hats off."

"We can't even get a picture," Jenna pointed out. "We don't have a camera! I have to return mine to the lab after each class."

"Jessie has a camera," Karen piped up. "A Polaroid."

Everyone turned to look at Jessie, who was leaning against the flagpole, staring off into space.

"You have a Polaroid camera?" Chelsea asked, nudging her.

Jessie blinked a few times as if she'd just woken up. "Oh . . . yeah. I forgot about that."

Jenna and Alex exchanged a glance. What a space case! She was holding onto the one item that might help them win, and she just forgot about it?

"Let's go!" Alex said.

Together the whole bunk ran back to their cabin. On the way they saw a bunch of boys from 2E trying to jump up and grab Nate's hat off his head. As far as Jenna could see, they didn't even have a camera, but it didn't matter, anyway. Nate was dodging and weaving and ducking and running. He wasn't letting them anywhere near his head. Back at 3C, Jessie dug through her cubby until she found the unused camera. Luckily there was a whole cartridge of film in it.

"Great. Now all we have to do is come up with a plan," Brynn said.

"What if we just tackle one of them?" Grace suggested breathlessly. "We could tackle Julie and hold her down and take her hat and—"

"I don't think we should gang-tackle Julie," Alex said. "We have to live with her for the rest of the summer. But we do have to get one of them down low so we can grab their hat."

"And then *we* need to get up high so we can take the picture," Valerie pointed out.

"We just need to get creative here, people," Alyssa said, biting her lip.

Get them down low and get us up high, Jenna thought.

Suddenly she was hit with a brilliant idea. "I've got it, you guys! I know what to do!"

▲ ▲ ▲

"Um . . . Jenna? Nat? Don't you think this is kind of dangerous?" Jessie whispered as they tiptoed their way through the storage room on the second floor of the main cabin.

"Come on, Jess! Don't you want to win?" Jenna asked, sidestepping a very dusty stack of ancient board games. What in the world was Uncle Wiggly, anyway?

"Yeah, but um . . . I'm kind of afraid of heights."

Outside, a bunch of girls squealed and a few

other people applauded. Time was running out. They had to get this last item before someone else won the scavenger hunt.

"Don't worry. Natalie and I will do it," Jenna said. "Right, Nat?"

"I grew up in a skyscraper," Natalie said, determined. "No problem."

They got to the window above the cabin's front porch, and Jenna undid the latch. Her pulse pounded in her ears, and she pulled up on the old window. It wouldn't budge.

"I don't think this thing has ever been opened," Jenna said.

"Here. Let's all try," Natalie suggested.

Together, the three girls gripped at the bottom of the old window and suddenly, without warning, it flew open, slamming into the top of the frame. Jenna and her friends froze, but luckily someone outside shouted at the exact same moment. It didn't seem like anyone down below had heard.

"No screen. Thank goodness," Jessie said.

"Okay, Nat. Let's go," Jenna said.

"Good luck, you guys!" Jessie whispered.

Jenna was the first to crawl out. She placed her foot on the roof of the porch's overhang and carefully put all her weight on it. The roof was sturdy as could be, and she realized she had been silly to worry. Matt had once told her that he and the other counselors sometimes snuck out here to look at the stars. Of course it would hold her.

"We're good. Come on," Jenna said to Natalie.

Natalie swung her leg over the windowsill and

followed Jenna out. They crept to the edge of the roof and lay down on their stomachs to stay out of sight. Jenna picked her head up carefully and saw Alex signal her from the trees across the way. Jenna lifted her hand in response, and Alex nodded.

"Here we go," she said to Natalie.

Giggling, they pulled themselves forward so they could see over the edge of the roof. Down below, Pete, Tyler, Marissa, and Stephanie were all hanging out, each wearing a baseball cap. A bunch of boys from 5F ran by, and the counselors cheered them on. They were followed by four very familiar faces.

"Here they come!" Natalie whispered.

Jenna held her breath. Valerie, Karen, Grace, and Chelsea all came running into view, right in front of the counselors. Val was holding the horseshoe again. A little touch to make it look real. It had been Alex's idea.

"Get ready," Natalie whispered.

Jenna propped the camera up and focused in on Tyler's head. One of these counselors was going down.

"We got it!" Valerie shouted again. "We got the last horseshoe!"

Just then, Karen tripped and fell right in the dirt in front of the counselors. Everyone stopped.

"Omigosh! Are you okay?" Chelsea asked.

And then, Karen started to wail. "My ankle! My ankle!" She even produced actual tears. Jenna and Natalie looked at each other. Little, quiet, mousy Karen was not a bad actress.

"She's like a secret weapon," Natalie said, her eyes bright.

"No joke," Jenna replied.

Instantly, all the counselors rushed to Karen's side. Tyler crouched down next to her and pulled her shoe off.

"Karen? Can you move it at all?" Marissa asked.

At that second, Alex and Sarah sprinted out of the trees across the way. Before anyone could even look up, Alex snatched the baseball cap off Tyler's head and Sarah got Pete's. Jenna snapped the picture, ripped the print from the side of the camera, then snapped another for good measure.

"Hey!" Pete shouted at Sarah.

"Where did you come from?" Tyler cried.

But Alex and Sarah were already sprinting away, followed by the rest of the bunk, who poured out of the trees, laughing and whooping all the way.

"Oh my God! We did it! I can't believe we did it!" Natalie cheered.

All the counselors looked up, and their jaws dropped when they saw Natalie and Jenna holding the camera triumphantly above their heads. Down below, Karen stood up, took a little bow, and raced off with Val, Grace, and Chelsea. Her ankle was totally fine.

"Hey! She didn't even hurt herself!" Pete shouted, picking up his hat from the ground where Sarah had tossed it. "Foul! Foul!"

But he was laughing. They all were. The counselors knew when they had been outsmarted, and they appreciated a game well-played.

Jenna held the pictures in front of her as they came into focus.

"Did they come out?" Jessie asked from the window.

"They're perfect!" Natalie announced. "We got

both of them!"

"We are so awesome!" Jenna cheered, and she and Natalie stood up and hugged. "Ha-ha! Bunk 3C rules!"

"Jenna Bloom!" Stephanie shouted up. "Get down from there! You'll kill yourself!"

"Oh, I'm coming down!" Jenna shouted back. "We have a scavenger hunt to win!"

chapter
EIGHT

By the time the bugle sounded to wake the camp the following morning, Jenna was still glowing from her bunk's scavenger hunt victory *and* she had a perfect prank in mind for Stephanie. The only problem was, she had no idea how she was going to pull it off. The planning was going to require some inside knowledge—some info even Jenna didn't have. And the even bigger problem was, the only people who could help her were the girls in Stephanie's bunk. The dreaded bunk 3A.

At breakfast, Jenna glanced over at the table where Stephanie was sitting with her campers, trying to figure out which one of the girls might help her. Danielle? No, everyone knew she was a total jerk. Christa? Not likely. That girl talked even less than Karen did. Ashley? No way. She had hated Jenna ever since Jenna planted that frog under her pillow two summers ago. Of course Jenna had only done it because 3A had short-sheeted all the beds in 3C. It was all just part of the rivalry.

"Jenna, why do you keep staring at 3A like that?" Alex asked toward the end of breakfast.

"She's probably trying to send them psychic 'I

hate you' messages," Grace joked, munching on her toast.

Brynn, Valerie, and Alex all giggled, throwing dirty looks at the other table. Jenna wasn't even sure when the war between the bunks had started. It was as if it had always been there.

"Oh! Leave the poor girls alone!" Brynn said, pretending to be sympathetic. "They're probably still all boo-hooing about how we beat them in the hunt last night."

"Yeah, we did!" Jenna cheered, high-fiving with her friends and letting out a little cheer. Bunk 3C had been the one and only bunk to get the bonus photo and had brought back the blue ribbon for the third year in a row. 3A had been on top until Jenna's bunk had raced in with the pictures just before the time had run out. Victory was sweet, but it was even sweeter when your lifelong enemies ended up moping all night.

"They're such losers," Alex said, rolling her eyes.

"I don't know. Some of them aren't that bad," Alyssa put in. "Like that girl Regina? She works on the paper with us, and she's really funny."

"Oh. My. Gosh. You did not just say that," Val said, dropping her hand to the table.

"Only a newbie would *ever* say that," Alex put in.

"You cannot like a 3A girl, Alyssa. It's, like, totally against the code," Chelsea said. Even though she was a newbie herself, she seemed to live for the rivalry as much as the veterans did.

"The code?" Natalie said with a laugh. "You sound like you're in the army or something."

"Well, pretend we are and they're the enemy," Brynn said. "Right, Jenna?"

Jenna looked guiltily at her friends. Normally, of course, she would be the first one talking about how annoying and jerky the 3A-ers were. But now, she needed them. Pretty soon one of her friends might even see her talking to them. What was she supposed to say?

"Well, *most* of them are awful," Jenna replied. "But not *all* of them."

"I can't believe I just heard Jenna Bloom say that," Alex said. "Do you have a fever or something?"

"Yeah, J, way to go against everything you've ever said. *Ever*," Sarah put in.

Jenna reddened and was relieved when breakfast was dismissed. Alex and Brynn rushed out, whispering, and Jenna knew they were talking about her and how she had turned on them. At the moment, she didn't care much, though. Jenna would do pretty much anything for a good prank, and that included letting her friends think she liked the girls in 3A. While the rest of her bunk trailed out the door, Jenna slowed her steps until bunk 3A caught up to her.

"Oh, look! It's a Bloom!" one of the veteran 3A girls, Sharon, said with a sneer.

"Oh, look! It's a slug!" Jenna shot back.

Two girls, including Regina from the paper, laughed at her joke, and Jenna realized that Alyssa was right. Regina was pretty cool. And her friend Marta had also been around forever, and had been in on some good raids. (Not as good as 3C's raids, but still good.) These two were definitely Jenna's best bets.

"Hey, Regina! Marta!" Jenna said, falling into step with them as they walked outside. "Can I talk to you?"

Regina glanced at Marta, who shrugged, and all

three of them stepped aside to let the other campers pass by.

"Listen, I want to pull a prank, and I need your help," Jenna whispered, glancing around.

"Our help?" Regina asked, tucking her short blond hair behind her ears. "Don't you have enough people in your own bunk?"

Even with the nicer, more normal girls, the bunk rivalry was strong.

"Yeah, but this prank only you guys can help me with," Jenna said. "I want to prank my sister."

"Stephanie? No way! We love Stephanie!" Marta said, pushing her big glasses up on her nose.

"I know! I do, too!" Jenna said, growing impatient already. She couldn't let too many people see her talking to girls from 3A. It was way too suspicious. "She's my sister. And I swear I wouldn't do anything to her if she didn't love pranks as much as I do," she added, crossing her fingers behind her back. "She'll think it's funny."

"I don't know . . ." Regina said, looking at Marta. Marta twisted a strand of her long black hair over her finger until her fingertip turned purple.

"Come on, you guys, it'll be fun," Jenna said. "And your bunkmates will think it's totally cool, right? Everyone loves a good prank."

Marta released her hair and started to smile slightly. Jenna knew she had her. The girl had some mischief in there somewhere. All Jenna had to do was wake it up.

"Well . . . what were you thinking of doing?" Marta asked.

Yes! Jenna thought. *Let the games begin!*

"You're absolutely sure she's in there? She always does her beauty routine on Sunday nights when we're at home," Jenna whispered on Friday afternoon. She, Regina, and Marta were all crouched below the back window of bunk 3A. Jenna had Jessie's Polaroid camera clutched in her sweaty hands, filled with film and ready to go. She had "borrowed" it out of Jessie's cubby, but was sure the girl would never notice. Aside from the scavenger hunt, she hadn't used it once all summer.

"Well, she's been doing it on Fridays ever since we got here. I promise. Every Friday during free swim," Regina said. She pressed her fingers into the ground to keep her wet bathing suit from hitting the dirt. They had all snuck out of free swim to do the deed, and Jenna could tell that the others were as nervous about getting caught as she was.

"Let's just do this and get back to the lake," Marta said, blinking rapidly.

"Okay, do one of you guys want to take the picture?" Jenna offered. "You got me the info, after all."

"No way. I don't know how to work that thing," Regina said.

"I can't even see without my glasses," Marta put in, swinging her long dark hair over her shoulder. "You're just a big yellow blur right now."

"Okay. Then I guess it's me," Jenna said, her heart slamming into her ribs. "Here goes nothing."

Jenna stood up and lifted the camera to her eye. The second she saw her sister, she almost cracked up laughing. Stephanie was lying on her cot a few feet from the window, her hair wrapped up in a towel, her face covered in a blue facial mask, with cucumber slices over her eyes. Where she got cucumbers out here, Jenna had no idea, but she was glad her sister was so resourceful. It made the picture all the more funny.

"Just take it!" Regina whispered.

Jenna quickly snapped the photo and hit the dirt. "Let's go!"

The girls got up and ran, giggling, all the way back to the edge of the path that led to the lake. By the time they got there, the photo had already developed. There, in full color, was Jenna's perfect sister, looking like some kind of creature from the black lagoon.

"Omigosh! It's so great!" Marta said.

"I thought you couldn't see," Jenna reminded her.

"Yeah, but I can imagine how great it is," Marta said.

Jenna rolled her eyes. "Do you have the note?"

"Here. I wrote it in my mother's handwriting so no one would know it was from me," Regina said, handing over a piece of Stephanie's own pink stationery.

"You can do your mother's handwriting?" Jenna asked, impressed.

"She never lets me go on class trips. I had to learn to do her signature," Regina said with a shrug.

Wow, Jenna thought. *Wish this girl was in* my *bunk.*

She quickly scanned the note:

Dear Tyler,
Roses are red,
Violets are blue,
I love cucumbers,

Hope you do, too!
Love,
Stephanie

"I love it!" Jenna squealed. Regina was *good*! "Now all we have to do is slip it into Tyler's bag. This is going to be so great."

"I hope Stephanie isn't too mad," Regina said, biting her bottom lip.

"Don't worry. She'll think it's funny. I swear," Jenna said, crossing her fingers again.

"I can't wait to see what happens next," Marta said with a grin.

Neither can I, Jenna thought, grinning. *I cannot wait.*

▲ ▲ ▲

That night all the campers in Jenna's year, along with their counselors and CITs, gathered by the lake to tell ghost stories. A campfire blazed on the sand, the lake shone in the moonlight, and the stars twinkled high overhead. All around them the woods were black as pitch. There wasn't a sound except for the crackling of the fire, the chirping crickets, and Pete's deep voice. Everyone was riveted by his story of the little old woman in the deserted house. Even people who heard it every year were still on the edge of their seats.

"The little old lady felt an icy chill creep down her back," Pete said in his most spooky voice. "All the tiny white hairs on her neck stood on end . . ."

Jenna, herself, felt like she was on red alert. Every nerve in her body was sizzling. But it was not because of

Pete's story. On the edge of the crowd were the CITs. Tyler was lounging back against the lifeguard's chair with some of the other guys while Stephanie and her friends sat on the old, overturned boat in the sand where the campers painted their bunk numbers at the end of each summer. Every once in a while Tyler would shoot a look at Stephanie, and every once in a while Stephanie would notice and smile back.

Tyler had to have seen the picture and the note. There was no way he could have missed it sitting right on top of his sunblock in his bag. Something was going to happen tonight. Jenna could feel it.

"Slowly . . . slowly . . . the little old lady crept toward the door," Pete said, the light from the fire dancing in his eyes and throwing eerie shadows across his face. "Step after step after step, she knew she might be walking to her doom . . ."

Suddenly Tyler pushed himself away from the lifeguard's chair. Jenna's heart hit her throat. Across the fire her eyes met Regina's, then Marta's. They were watching, too. They were all dying to know what was going to happen.

Stephanie saw Tyler coming. She stood up a little straighter, tossed her hair behind one shoulder, and smiled slyly at Marissa.

"Her gnarled old fingers shook with fear as she reached for the doorknob . . ."

Tyler's hand went to his pocket. He pulled something out. The envelope! The pink envelope!

"Her hand grasped the cool brass handle. She closed her eyes and said a prayer . . ."

Stephanie blinked in confusion. She took the

envelope and opened it. Her face went white as she saw the picture. The envelope fluttered to the sand. Jenna looked at Regina and slapped her hand over her mouth to keep from laughing. Marta already had her face buried in Regina's back, her shoulders shaking.

"The little old lady opened the door and—"

"*What is this!?*" Stephanie shrieked at the top of her lungs.

All the campers around the fire jumped. Jenna saw Natalie grab Simon out of fear, then flush and look away. Even Adam looked like he had just seen a ghost.

"Who did this!?" Stephanie shouted, kicking up sand as she stalked toward the fire.

"Stephanie, come on," Tyler pleaded, following her. "It's no big deal. I mean, I knew it was a joke."

It seemed like Stephanie hadn't even heard him. She stepped into the center of the circle and glared at the girls in her cabin, holding the photo up.

"I know it had to be one of you!" she shouted. "You're the only ones who know when I use my mask. So who did it, huh? Who took this picture?"

Still barely containing her laughter, Jenna glanced at Regina and Marta again. But now, neither one of them was laughing. They both looked upset and guilty. Regina turned accusing eyes toward Jenna, and Jenna knew what she was thinking. She had promised Regina that Stephanie would think the prank was funny. And from the way Stephanie was reacting, it was clear that that was not the case.

"No one has the guts to confess?" Stephanie asked.

There was total silence aside from the crackling of the fire.

"Fine," Stephanie said, clenching her jaw. "I'm outta here."

Then she turned and stalked through the circle and headed back for the bunks. Marissa got up and ran after her, and Tyler shrugged. "Well, I thought it was funny," he said, causing a quick round of laugher and breaking the tension.

Jenna leaned back on her elbows and sighed happily. Forget Regina and Marta. It wasn't her fault they didn't have the stomach for a good joke. As far as she was concerned, it was another successful prank. At least Jenna Bloom was still good at something.

chapter
NINE

Jenna could not believe her luck. She was sitting at the social planning committee meeting after dinner on Monday and there were more than a dozen kids sitting around her, boys and girls from every age group. But not one of them was a brother or sister. Stephanie and Adam were both absent. She was actually the only Bloom on the committee.

"What's with the freaky big smile?" Chelsea asked her.

"Just happy to be here," Jenna said with a shrug as Shira, the camp's events coordinator, welcomed them.

Shira was an ever-peppy college student who always wore shirts with Greek letters on them. She had curly black hair, a huge smile, and could talk faster than anyone Jenna had ever met. Just then she was babbling on about how they should all be honored to be part of such an important event.

"Okay, the first thing we need to decide on is a theme for the event," Shira said, once she was done with her welcome speech. Her crazy black curls framed her face as she looked up at the table. Her pink-ink pen was poised above a bright green clipboard, ready to take suggestions. "Any ideas? I know you kids are just bursting with creativity!"

"How about *The Lord of the Rings?*" a boy from 3E suggested. He had a cowlick the size of New Jersey and wore a faded Frodo T-shirt.

"Nice!" Pete cheered. He, Nate, and a couple of other counselors were hanging out by the wall, listening in on the meeting.

"Um . . . interesting, but not exactly appropriate for a social," Shira said, shooting Pete a look. "Good start, though. Anyone else?"

"Hey, I liked it, buddy," Pete said, leaning over to slap the Frodo kid on the back. The Frodo kid turned fire-engine red and slumped a little bit, crossing his arms on the table.

"We could do Hollywood," Chelsea put in, sitting up straight. "We could have a red carpet, and stars hanging from the ceiling and stuff like that."

"Ooh! That could be so glam and romantic," an older girl said with a grin.

"I like it!" Shira said. "Anyone else?"

Romantic? Yuck! Jenna thought, looking around as some of the younger kids squirmed. *Who wants romance? Well, besides all my crazy friends who are going with dates.*

"What about a square dance?" a fifth-year girl named Gwendolyn suggested. "We could learn all the different dances and maybe we could have a competition for the best dancers."

Jenna sat up a little straighter at this idea. A square dance competition sounded like a lot more fun, and a lot less "romantic" than Chelsea's Hollywood idea.

"A square dance! How fun!" Shira trilled, scribbling

on her clipboard. "We could get bales of hay and horseshoes and cowboy hats. Great idea, Gwen!"

"A square dance? That's so third grade," Chelsea said, brushing the idea off.

The third-graders at the table sank lower in their chairs, and Jenna elbowed Chelsea in the ribs. Jenna still remembered how annoying it was when older kids had brushed *her* ideas off just because she was younger.

"Ow!" Chelsea said.

"I think it's a great idea," Jenna put in, covering up Chelsea's complaints. "It would be a lot of fun. Like, all bright and happy and stuff."

"Yeah, and learning the dances would be cool," another girl put in.

"Would we *have* to dance?" the Frodo boy asked.

"Not if you don't want to," Jenna said. "But if you wanted to, you would be matched up with someone as your partner. You know, for the contest. Right?"

Frodo Boy actually brightened. "So I could actually dance without having to go up to a girl and ask her? I like *that* idea."

"Jenna's got a good point," Nate said. "A square dance is actually perfect."

Jenna felt a little flutter in her heart as she beamed. Nate was agreeing with her! One of the coolest counselors at camp!

"Come on!" one of the older girls said. "A square dance is silly."

"Hey!" Gwen replied.

"Everyone calm down and listen to what Nate has to say," Shira suggested. "Nate?"

"Well, whenever we have one of these things,

all the girls stand on one side of the room, and all the boys stand on the other side, and it takes half the night for anyone to get up the guts to ask anyone else to dance," Nate said. "If we do the square dance, everyone will be dancing all night. I think it would be much more relaxed."

Exactly what I was thinking, Jenna thought with a smile. "Plus, lately everyone has felt all this pressure to come with a date," Jenna said, thinking of how serious Grace had been when she had made Jenna promise to go solo. "If everyone knows they're going to get to dance with someone even if they *don't* already have a date, then everyone could, you know, chill about it."

"Well put," Shira said. "Well, we have two theme ideas. Let's put it to a vote. All for the Hollywood theme?"

Chelsea and a bunch of the older girls and guys raised their hands. Shira counted quickly and made a note on her board.

"And all for the square-dance theme?" she asked.

Jenna, Gwen, Frodo Boy, and all the younger kids, plus Nate and the rest of the counselors raised their hands. Shira counted again, but it was already clear which idea had won.

"Square dance it is!"

Yes! Jenna thought as a few kids cheered and clapped. Nate grinned at her, and she felt as if she were on top of the world. This was going to be the coolest camp dance-social-thingie ever.

"I can't believe you actually voted for that square-dance idea," Chelsea grumbled as they headed back to their bunk later that night, a few paces behind the group of older girls. "Why don't we just have a diaper theme?"

"Come on, Chelsea! It'll be fun!" Jenna said.

Jenna knew Chelsea was just upset that her idea had been outvoted, but the square dance was such a better idea. It was more important that the entire camp have a fun social than it was to keep Chelsea happy.

"Yeah, bales of hay, cornbread and beans, and a bunch of uncoordinated boys bouncing up and down," Chelsea said, pausing in front of the nature shack. "Yee-ha."

"Chelsea . . ."

"It's my first date ever, and now I'm always going to remember that Eric took me to a hoedown," she said.

"What's the big deal? You still get to dance with him," Jenna said. "Even thought I still can't figure out *why* you want to."

"Whatever, Jenna. You just don't get it yet," Chelsea said. "But one day you're gonna want to go out with a boy. I swear."

"Not unless somebody sucks my brain out and replaces it with yours," Jenna said.

Chelsea scoffed. She glanced behind her at the nature shack, then looked at Jenna with a sly smile.

"You know what? It's too bad there aren't any animals for our Old McDonald's farm dance," she said. "That would just make the whole thing *perfect*."

With that, Chelsea walked off, huffily stomping along the pathway toward the bunks. Jenna, however, couldn't make herself move. Was Chelsea suggesting what Jenna thought she was suggesting? Whether or not

Chelsea had realized it, she had started a brilliant idea forming in Jenna's mind. She stared at the nature shack, her wicked brain already putting together the details.

Animals for Old McDonald's Farm . . .

She couldn't. She shouldn't. Especially not after the way Stephanie had reacted to the last prank. She should be hanging up her thinking cap for the rest of the summer and leaving the pranks to the other kids. Besides, if she kept it up, sooner or later she was going to get caught. And if she got caught, her parents would wig out—not to mention her brother Matt, who had made her promise to be good.

But it would just be so totally amazing! It would be the biggest, most creative, most legendary prank ever pulled in the history of Camp Lakeview. Jenna would be talked about for years. Everyone would know her name. If she could pull it off, she would be Jenna the Champion Prankster, not just another Bloom.

It really is a good idea, Jenna thought, smiling. *A really good*, bad *idea* . . .

▲ ▲ ▲

"Okay, I'm totally bored," Jenna said, slumping back in her chair at the newspaper.

She looked at Natalie and Alyssa, who were busy going through a stack of photographs for the next issue. All around the room, campers huddled over desks, tapped away at the two ancient computers or flipped through old issues of the camp paper—*The Acorn*—for ideas. Various bulletin boards hung on the walls displayed unused pictures of campers from every age group, eating lunch, playing volleyball, smiling for the camera. But even with all the activity inside the cabin, it still felt stifling just to be there. Jenna could hear the squeals and shouts of the kids playing soccer on the field outside and was practically green with jealousy.

"Do we really need to print a list of all the competitions and who's won them?" Jenna asked, tossing her pen down and stretching out her aching fingers. The fan in the corner swung slowly in their direction, and she lifted her ponytail to feel the cool air on the back of her neck. It actually seemed hotter in here than it was outside. Why wasn't she out in the sun kicking a soccer ball around right now instead of being cooped up inside doing busy work?

Natalie stopped tapping her red pencil against the edge of the long wooden table and smirked at Jenna. "I thought you would love doing that list. Your name is on it, like, at least five times."

"Yeah. You're like Queen of Camp Lakeview," Alyssa put in.

Jenna couldn't help smiling at the compliment and almost wished Alex were there to hear it. She did have to admit, her name and her bunk appeared very often on the rundown she was working on. Bunk 3C had not only won the scavenger hunt, but they were in the semifinals of the summerlong capture-the-flag-tournament and had won the girls' kickball competition. Jenna herself had taken home the blue ribbon in the obstacle course in her age division and second place in the cross-country race (just behind Sarah). It *was* kind of cool getting so much recognition. Maybe putting this list together wasn't as boring as she had thought.

"Okay, but when I'm done with this, I get to do something fun," Jenna said, sitting up again. She sifted through the stack of slips on which the counselors had written their campers' many triumphs. Even though Julie's slip had Jenna's name all over it, the list couldn't record Jenna's biggest news of the summer. She had pulled two huge pranks, and no one had figured out it was her! That should have been front-page news.

"Hey! Maybe I'll write a story about all the pranks that have been going on!" Jenna suggested.

Natalie and Alyssa exchanged a look as the newspaper supervisor, Keith, walked by. Keith was Nate's older brother and had been a counselor at Lakeview until a couple of years ago. He worked on a computer magazine in South Jersey and was going to be some big reporter one day. He looked just like Nate, only taller, skinnier, and nerdier.

"I don't think that's such a good idea, Jenna," Keith said, pausing by their table. His thick glasses hung on the edge of his nose, making him look like an owl.

"Why not?" Jenna asked. "It's an interesting story. And funny. I mean, you guys think those pranks were funny . . . right?" she asked her friends.

"Yeah . . . sure," Alyssa responded slowly, looking away.

"I understand why you think it would be a fun story, Jenna, but this issue is for parents' day," Keith said. "I don't think the parents really want to hear about pranks being pulled on their kids, do you?"

Jenna flushed slightly. The only parents who would be reading about pranks pulled on their kids would be her own. After all, the only pranks so far this year had been pulled on Adam and Stephanie. And Keith was right. Her parents would not want to hear about those jokes. Not this summer, especially.

"All right," Jenna grumbled, never too willing to give up, even when she knew she should. "But I think you should check the Constitution. I know there's something about the press being able to write whatever they want."

Keith smiled. "Well, not *whatever* they want, but that's a lesson for another day."

Jenna sighed and returned to her repetitive task, wincing when she heard a huge cheer from outside. Someone had clearly scored a goal. Jenna was missing all the fun.

"Oooh! I *love* this one," Alyssa said, holding up a picture across the way. "It's so artistic."

"Totally," Natalie agreed. "Who took it?"

Alyssa flipped the photo over. "Adam Bloom," she read, sounding surprised. "Hey, Jenna, your brother's a great photographer."

Jenna looked up from her work. "Let me see," she said, sure it was going to be some random picture of Adam's friends making faces or something.

Alyssa turned the photo around and held it up for Jenna to see. It was a shot of the lake at sunset with the light reflecting all the trees in the water. Even Jenna had to admit it was totally gorgeous. It was like something a person could frame and hang on the wall.

"Wow," she said, burning with jealousy. "That *is* good. But you can't use that for the paper, right? I mean, there are no campers in it and it doesn't show an activity, so what's the point?"

"Oh, well, Keith said we could print some of the

more artsy shots in the parents' day edition," Natalie said, placing Adam's photo aside. "You know, to show off to the parents what we're doing at camp."

"Yeah. We're picking out the best ones," Alyssa said.

Jenna shifted in her seat, staring at Adam's photo. "Oh. So you're picking that one?"

"Definitely," Alyssa said. "That's the best one yet."

"Hey! You're in photography now, right?" Natalie said, her eyes bright. "Why don't you hand in some of your pictures?"

Jenna pressed her pen into the page in front of her, scowling. "I don't think so," she said. Natalie and Alyssa had no idea that Jenna had basically underexposed, blurred, or blackened out almost all of her pictures when she'd tried to print them. She just couldn't seem to get that machine to work right.

"Why not?" Alyssa asked. "If Adam's are this good, yours are probably awesome. I mean, he *is* your brother."

"Yeah! Maybe it's in your blood!" Natalie added with a grin.

"My pictures stink, all right?" Jenna said flatly. "Can we please talk about something else?"

Natalie and Alyssa fell silent for a moment. A long moment that seemed to drag out forever. Jenna couldn't believe she had snapped at her friends again. What was she doing—turning into an even jerkier version of Chelsea or something?

"Hey! I know what we can talk about!" Alyssa said finally, glancing around the room as if to check if anyone was watching. Jenna leaned forward, curious, as Alyssa bent down and rummaged through her black messenger bag. "Check it out," she said, lifting a small box just into view at the end of the table. Jenna's eyes nearly popped out of her head. It was a box of hair dye. Red hair dye.

"Who is that for?" Jenna asked as Alyssa slipped the box out of sight again.

"For me," Alyssa said, grinning wildly.

Jenna stared at Alyssa's long black locks. She couldn't believe she was actually thinking about dyeing her hair! Alyssa had always been a little . . . *different*, what with her wardrobe of ripped jeans, paint-spattered cargo shorts, and black T-shirts. But this? This was totally off the deep end!

"Where did you get it?" Jenna asked.

"That senior girl Daphne gave it to us," Natalie said, lifting her chin toward the other end of the room. "Plus, the bleach we have to use first."

"Bleach?" Jenna said, her mouth dropping open. "Are you crazy?"

"Daphne says she does it all the time," Alyssa replied. "It's no big deal."

Jenna turned around to check out Daphne, a thirteen-year-old girl with white-blond hair. She was sitting at a table in the back of the room, chopping up newspapers with a pair of huge scissors. Jenna wasn't sure what good her task was doing anyone, but as always, no one was bothering her. Daphne had been wearing black eyeliner ever since Jenna could remember, and whenever anyone asked her a question, she just grunted. She also cracked her knuckles constantly. Jenna had always been totally afraid of Daphne. Most of the *counselors* were even afraid of her. How had Natalie and Alyssa even gotten her to *talk* to them?

"She changes her hair color every five minutes," Natalie said.

"Yeah, wasn't she a brunette last week?" Jenna asked.

"Yep," Alyssa said. "She was saving the red for the end of the summer, but I traded her my pastel set for it. I wanted to do something cool and different for the social."

"Wow. Well, it'll definitely be different," Jenna said. "So, when are we going to do it?"

"Tonight," Natalie whispered. "It's Julie's night off, and you know Marissa sleeps like she's practically dead or something," she added with a giggle.

"Aren't you afraid of getting in trouble?" Jenna asked Alyssa.

"It's never stopped you, has it?" Alyssa said with a grin.

Jenna grinned back. How cool! She was inspiring Alyssa to take a chance! "No, I guess not."

"Besides, what are they going to do to me?" Alyssa asked with a shrug. "By the time they see what I've done, it'll be too late. And it is *my* hair."

They could do a lot of things to you, Jenna thought. *Like give you extra chores or make you help out in the mess hall.* Jenna had gotten enough punishments in her life to know that Alyssa could get in big trouble. But still, it was cool to see how calm Alyssa was about it all.

"Wow," Jenna said, leaning back in her chair again. "I'm impressed."

"And she's going to look so *fabb*-u-lous with red highlights," Natalie said, fluttering her lashes and tilting her head back.

"Thank you, *dah*-ling," Alyssa replied, flipping her hair.

Jenna giggled, her boredom and irritation over Adam and his pictures entirely forgotten. Tonight was going to be so much fun. And for once, she wasn't going to be the one getting yelled at or having suspicious looks thrown at her. For once, something big was going to happen, and no one would be able to blame it on her.

Dear Matt,

    I can't believe you think it was me who pulled the pranks on Stephanie and Adam. First of all, they're total whiners for telling you about them, anyway, because they were no big deal. But just because I am the "common link" (your words) between them, that doesn't mean I did it. Besides, the sugar prank was pulled on Adam's entire table, not just Adam. How do you know someone wasn't trying to prank Eric? Or Simon? Or Nate?

    Besides, you know that if it WAS

me, I wouldn't be able to tell you, anyway. The less people that know you did a prank, the better—right? And when did you get so parental? Wasn't it you who replaced the morning bugle sound track with "You Gotta Fight for Your Right to Party" that summer? People still talk about that. And you KNOW you love it.

Just in case you're interested in the good things I'm doing this summer, we won the scavenger hunt AGAIN, and I'm on the planning committee for the camp social. It's going to be the best one ever. And Mom and Dad still haven't gotten any freak-out phone calls. So there.

I hope you're having fun with your beakers and test tubes!

Love,
Jenna

P.S. Thanks for the "I Eat Glue" bumper sticker. Very funny, you know, since I actually used to eat glue. Yum! Ha-ha. I swear I don't eat glue anymore.

That night, after lights-out, Julie left to meet up with the other counselors and do whatever it was they did on their nights off. *Probably a lot of kissing and holding hands*, Jenna thought. *Gross.*

Jenna lay in her top bunk, staring at the ceiling, holding her breath and listening to the sound of her heartbeat. In the other bunks the rest of her friends were doing the same. Jenna turned her face and stole a glance at Valerie who grinned back. Everyone was psyched for what they were about to do.

The minutes dragged on for what seemed like days, but soon enough Jenna heard the soft whistle of Marissa's snoring. Somewhere in the bunk someone snorted a laugh and clapped her hand over her mouth. Jessie and Karen giggled and twittered until Alex shushed them. Finally the tiny beeping alarm on Sarah's sports watch went off, and everyone sat up. Fifteen minutes had passed. Nothing but the trumpet reveille could wake Marissa now.

Ever so quietly Jenna slipped from her bed and down the ladder, bumping butts with Alex as she came down from her own.

"Are you ready?" Grace asked Alyssa as they all

gathered in the center of the bunk in socked-feet.

"Yeah. Let's do this," Alyssa said.

"Yeah," Candace added. "Let's do this."

A few of the girls giggled and started to whisper.

"Shhh! No more talking till we're in the bathroom!" Jenna hissed, causing everyone to immediately shut up. Jenna smiled, happy she had come up with the order before Alex, and they all tiptoed past Marissa's cot and into the bathroom.

Brynn went for the light, but Alex grabbed her hand to stop her.

"Pull the curtain first!" Alex said in a whisper.

Jessie yanked the burgundy curtain across the door opening to shield some of the light from spilling into the bunk area, and then Brynn flicked the light on. Alyssa, Natalie, Valerie, and Grace were already gathered at the back sink.

"This is going to be so cool!" Natalie said, tearing the box open. It made a hugely loud noise, and Jenna's heart jumped into her throat. Everyone looked at the door. When they heard Marissa snore again, they let out a big sigh of relief.

"She's in dreamland," Chelsea said. "Don't worry about her."

"Okay, we've already read the directions about ten times," Natalie said. "Let's just go for it."

"Are you sure you want to do this, Alyssa?" Alex asked, ever the cautious camper. She looked at Alyssa's reflection in the mirror, and Alyssa gazed steadily back.

"I'm sure," she said with a nod. "Let's go."

"I can't believe we're doing this. I can't believe we're doing this!" Grace babbled excitedly.

Jenna grabbed one of Alyssa's towels and draped it over her shoulders. Natalie wiggled her fingers into the plastic gloves while Grace removed the safety cap from the bottle of dye. Valerie used a comb to help Natalie work parts into Alyssa's hair. Then Natalie held up the dye bottle.

"This is it!" Natalie said with a grin. Alyssa nodded quickly, and Natalie applied the dye. After a few seconds of watching them work, a sharp, sour smell hit Jenna's nostrils, and she scrunched her nose.

"Ugh! That stuff smells gross!" she whispered.

"Sometimes you have to suffer for beauty," Natalie replied, still working. "Or at least that's what my dad's girlfriend always says."

Everyone nodded at this piece of wisdom. Natalie's dad was Ted Maxwell, the huge Hollywood star. His current girlfriend, Josie McLaughlan, was a starlet on the rise who had appeared on the cover of nearly every women's magazine last spring. If anyone knew about beauty, she did.

"Everything okay out there, Karen?" Valerie asked, glancing toward the door.

Karen moved the curtain slightly and peeked out. "Yep," she whispered with a nod. "She's still asleep."

"Okay," Natalie said when the bottle of dye was empty. "Now we just wait fifteen minutes and rinse it out."

Sarah pressed a few buttons on her watch and nodded. "Okay. Timer's set."

Jenna looked around the bathroom. What were they going to do for fifteen minutes? With no other options in sight, she finally shrugged and sat down on the rough wooden floor. The other girls soon joined her and they all sat in a circle, breathing in the fumes from Alyssa's head.

"How does it feel?" Jenna asked.

"It burns a little, but the box said it would," Alyssa replied calmly. Jenna couldn't believe how brave she was, sitting there like there was nothing going on. If Jenna was changing the color of her own hair, she would be losing it right then.

"I can't wait to see how it looks," Grace said.

"Me neither," Jessie put in. "I just read the part in *Anne of Green Gables* where she tries to dye her red hair black and it comes out all green and horrible . . ."

Everyone stared at Jessie until she realized what she was saying and all the color drained from her face.

"Not that your hair's going to be green and horrible," she added quickly. "I'm sure it's gonna look great."

Jenna rolled her eyes and leaned back on her hands. Sometimes Jessie could say the most spacey things. There was a moment of awkward silence, which Grace finally broke.

"I love the movie version of *Anne of Green Gables*," she said. "Actually I think it was a miniseries. My mom bought it for me on tape."

"Have you read the book?" Jessie asked.

Grace flushed slightly. "No . . . just seen the movie."

"Oh, well, the book is *so* much better," Jessie said. "I can lend it to you if you want."

"That's okay," Grace said.

"Actually, you kind of look like Anne, Grace," Karen said. "Your hair is the exact same color as hers."

"Really? Well, soon Alyssa's gonna look like her, too!" Grace announced, bringing the attention back to the hair dye at hand.

"I was actually hoping for more punk rock than prairie-girl chic," Alyssa said.

Everyone laughed, and after that they pretty much stayed quiet until the beeper on Sarah's watch went off again.

"Time to rinse!" Natalie said, jumping up.

Alyssa scrambled to her feet and followed Natalie to the sink. She dipped her head forward under the spout.

"How does it look?" Alyssa asked. Her eyes were scrunched shut to keep the dye out.

Jenna's mouth was totally dry. The water pouring from Alyssa's hair and down the drain was bright red, like the color of blood. It was totally gross. Jenna was really worried. If Alyssa's hair was the same color as that water, she wasn't going to look as *fabb*-u-lous as Natalie had predicted at the newspaper. She was going to look *scary*.

"It's . . . hard to tell," Grace said. "Because, you know, your hair is still wet and the color always looks different when it's wet."

"So let's dry it," Chelsea said, pulling her hairdryer out. The girls all kept their toiletries in plastic crates near the wall and Chelsea's was on the top shelf, always overflowing with headbands, barrettes, and various ribbons.

"No!" Alex whispered. "You can't turn that on!"

"She's right," Alyssa said, lifting her head and wrapping the towel from her shoulders around her hair. "I know Marissa's a deep sleeper, but that could definitely wake her up."

Jenna felt as disappointed as the rest of her friends looked. "So what do we do?" she asked.

"We just wait until the morning," Alyssa said. "It'll dry overnight."

"Wow. Can you really wait that long?" Jenna asked. There was no way she would be as calm as Alyssa was right then. Dyeing her hair was a huge thing! How could she not be freaking out?

"I kind of have to," Alyssa said, leading the way to the door. "Come on, girls, let's get some sleep. Tomorrow you'll get to see the whole new me!"

▲ ▲ ▲

The next morning Jenna woke up super early, just like she always did on Christmas morning. For a moment she couldn't figure out why she was so excited, and then she remembered. Alyssa's top bunk was across the room from Jenna's, so she rolled over to take a look. Maybe she could be the first person to get a look at the hair! Unfortunately, Alyssa must have been sleeping all the way back against the wall. All Jenna could see was her blanket and the edge of her pillow.

As patiently as she could, Jenna waited until reveille. She must have dozed off again, because when the trumpet went off, she sat up so fast, she smacked her head into the ceiling.

Alex, Chelsea, and Natalie, always up before the trumpet, all ran in from the bathroom. The rest of the girls shot one another glances from their bunks, grinning with anticipation. Finally Alyssa, the second heaviest sleeper next to Marissa, sat up and swung her feet over the side of the bunk.

Jenna let out a gasp that was echoed by the rest of

the girls. Suddenly she felt sick to her stomach. Alyssa's hair, all knotted and stringy from being slept on wet, was Ronald McDonald red!

"What?" Alyssa said, her eyes still closed as she stretched her arms out at her sides.

"Alyssa! Your . . . your hair!" Natalie wailed.

Suddenly Alyssa's eyes popped open, and her hands flew to her head. She grabbed her long hair and slowly brought the ends in front of her face. Her eyes widened to the size of softballs.

"Omigod!" she gasped, sliding down off her bunk and dropping to the floor. She ran to the bathroom, followed by the rest of the bunk, and stared into the mirror. "Oh . . . my . . . God!"

It looked even worse in the bright lights of the bathroom. Alyssa's hair wasn't just red. It was flaming, fire-engine, hot-sauce, ketchup red. She looked like a Raggedy Ann doll. All around her reflection were the faces of her eleven stunned bunkmates. It was clear to Jenna that no one knew what to say. It was Natalie who finally broke the silence.

"Alyssa, I am so, so, so, so sorry," she said, holding her hands over her mouth. "I swear I followed the directions. I don't know what happened."

Alyssa was just opening her mouth to say something when Julie walked into the room, all smiles in her gray sweats and white T-shirt. All the campers froze in place.

We are so dead, Jenna thought. *So very, very dead.*

"Good morning, girls!" Julie said, grabbing her toothbrush and taking it over to the sink. "Are you guys ready for another beautiful—ACK!!!"

Julie dropped her toothbrush in the sink with a clatter and whirled to face the little group of campers. Everyone tightened in around Alyssa as if to protect her.

"What happened?" Julie asked. "What did you do to yourself?"

"I . . . I . . . dyed it," Alyssa said, looking at the floor.

"With what? Paint from the arts-and-crafts cabin?" Julie cried. She reached out and took a few strands in her hand. "Oh, Alyssa, what were you thinking?"

"I thought it was just going to be highlights!" Alyssa said, lifting her big brown eyes to look at Julie. "I didn't know!"

Julie sighed and put her hands on her hips. "Did you girls help her do this?" she asked, looking around.

"No!" Alyssa piped up immediately. "They didn't even know until this morning."

"Lyss," Natalie said.

"I swear, Julie. If anyone should get in trouble, it should just be me," Alyssa said, turning to look in the mirror again. "Ugh! I look like a horror movie!"

Julie sighed again and shook her head. "All right, everyone but Alyssa, back outside," she said, pointing a thumb at the door.

Everyone shot sympathetic looks at Alyssa. On top of looking like an oversized rag doll, she was about to get in major trouble. It didn't seem fair. Back outside the bathroom, Jenna and Alex both hovered near the door to hear.

"Alyssa, why did you do this?" Julie asked, her voice low.

"I thought it would be cool for the social tonight," Alyssa replied.

"And who gave you the dye?" Julie asked.

There was a pause. "No one. I brought it with me to camp."

Wow. Alyssa's a good person to have on your side, Jenna thought, sharing a look with Alex. *She's not even giving Daphne up.*

"Well, technically, I should revoke your privileges and at least make you stay home from the social," Julie said, causing Jenna and Alex to gasp. "But I won't," she added.

"Really?" Alyssa said.

"I think looking at your reflection for the rest of the summer will be punishment enough," Julie said. "Now go tell your friends you're not in trouble. Except for the two nosy nosersons standing by the door, because they already know."

Caught, Jenna and Alex jumped back and joined the rest of their friends to wait for Alyssa to come out.

"I'm not in trouble!" Alyssa shouted, throwing her hands in the air.

Everyone cheered and started to go about getting ready for breakfast. Natalie, Grace, and Alyssa huddled in the corner, brushing out Alyssa's hair and trying to figure out a way to make it look better. In the end, they borrowed a baseball cap from Sarah and decided to deal with it later.

As Jenna headed for the sink to wash her face and brush her teeth, her mind was working overtime. She couldn't believe Alyssa hadn't gotten in trouble. If Jenna had dyed her own hair, she was sure Julie would have sent her right to Dr. Steve. Jenna *always* got in trouble when she was caught.

Or maybe not, she thought, looking at her reflection in the mirror. Maybe Julie was softening a little. And there hadn't been any big drama over either one of her last pranks. As far as Jenna knew, the camp director and the counselors still didn't know for sure who had pulled them. Maybe the whole camp was getting a little easier on pranksters and jokesters. If Alyssa could turn herself into a clown and not get in trouble, there was no telling what Jenna might be able to get away with.

Tonight was the social, and she could still pull the all-time greatest prank . . . if she dared. Sizzling with excitement, Jenna brushed her teeth quickly and headed outside for some alone time while everyone else got ready. She had a lot of thinking to do. Tonight, Jenna Bloom could become a legend.

That night, the social was in full swing in the mess hall and all the campers seemed to be having a great time. Jenna hung back against the wall behind the huge punch bowl and took in the scene. Nate had been right. Instead of everyone being divided, boys against one wall and girls against the other, most of the kids were in the center of the floor, laughing while the counselors tried to teach them some square-dance moves. A lot of the girls had done their hair in double braids, and many of them had tracked down plaid and denim clothing to go along with the theme. Some of the boys were wearing brown plastic cowboy hats that Pete had found at a local party store, and Julie stood in the corner, handing out colorful bandannas for the campers to tie around their necks.

Bales of hay were stacked against the walls and around the snack tables. Silver and gold stars were hanging from the ceiling—the only idea left over from Chelsea's Hollywood plan. But now they were stars of the desert night instead of stars of L.A. There were even a few inflatable cacti leaning against the DJ table where Pete played old square dance records someone had dug up from the AV room. Everything had come together just as the planning committee had dreamed it.

"Hey, Jenna! Aren't you going to dance!?" Natalie called out as Simon grabbed her arm and swung her around. Natalie tipped her head back and laughed, and Jenna couldn't help but smile. Nat looked like she was having an amazing time.

"Maybe later," Jenna said. "I'm in charge of punch right now!"

Natalie waved and twirled away. Jenna looked down at her lavender dress and sighed. She wasn't actually in charge of punch. The punch could take care of itself. The problem for Jenna was, she just couldn't get into party mode. It turned out that dancing with boys, even silly square dancing, was not her thing. The very thought of letting one of Adam's grubby friends spin her around and grab her hand made her cringe.

But everyone else seemed to be enjoying it, so what was wrong with Jenna? She always had fun at the camp dance, even when she just spent the night talking to her friends. What was wrong with her this year?

Jenna saw Adam approaching the punch table and pushed herself away from the wall. She went about filling cups from the punch bowl, trying to look important and busy.

"Hey, Jen," he said, pausing in front of her. He looked kind of pale and tired, but that was what he got for spending half his summer in the darkroom. Adam may have been good with photos, but he was going to go back to school in September looking like a vampire.

"What's up?" Jenna said, lifting the ladle from the bowl.

"You having fun?" he asked. He fiddled with the cord

that held the plastic cowboy hat that hung down his back.

"Sure," she said. "You?"

"I guess," Adam said, scanning the room. "So . . . listen, who's that new girl in your bunk? The one with the red hair?"

For a moment, Jenna thought of Grace, who had red curly hair. But she had been new *last* year and Adam knew her. She followed his gaze across the room and her jaw dropped. Adam was staring at Alyssa, who was standing by the far wall chatting with Daphne. Alyssa had her tomato-red mop pulled back in a ponytail and had made a belt by tying five of the multicolored bandannas together. Alyssa probably thought she looked cool, but Jenna thought the outfit just made her look even more like a clown.

Jenna glanced back at Adam. He looked as if he had stars in his eyes. He could have been that old cartoon skunk whose heart always thumped out his chest whenever he saw that black-and-white girl cat. Oh, God! Did Adam have a *crush?* On one of her *friends?* Could this summer get any worse?

"Jenna? Are you in there?" Adam asked.

"That's Alyssa," Jenna said finally. "She's from south Jersey and she just did that to her hair last night. Kind of bright, right?" she said, attempting a laugh. She felt bad for picking on Alyssa to her brother, but she didn't want Adam to like Alyssa. She *really* didn't want that. She already shared *everything* with her brothers and sister. Was she going to have to share her friends, too?

"Actually, I think it's kind of cool," Adam said. "Is she into art?"

Jenna swallowed hard. "Why do you say that?"

"She has paint all over her sneakers," Adam pointed out.

"So what? You like artsy girls all of a sudden?" Jenna asked. "Why? Because you're such an *amazing photographer* now?"

Adam looked at her like he felt sorry for her. "You could be, too, you know, if you just paid attention to what you were doing."

"Well, maybe I'm not into lame-o photography," Jenna shot back. "I'd rather be playing kickball than sitting in that cave all darn day."

"Okay! Okay! Forget I said anything," Adam replied, raising his hands in surrender. "So, what's Alyssa into? What are her electives?"

"Uh . . . she's on the paper with me and she's in arts and crafts," Jenna said, filling another cup. "You don't, like, really *like* her, do you?"

"I don't know," Adam said, re- :hing back and placing his cowboy hat firmly on his head. "Let's find out!" he said with a smile.

Oh, ick! Jenna thought, watching as Adam walked across the room and struck up a conversation with Alyssa. She couldn't have looked away if she'd tried. This couldn't be happening. Adam couldn't be crushing on one of her bunkmates. If Adam and Alyssa got together it would be such a nightmare! Her brother would be in her face even more than he already was.

And why this summer of all summers? Why was this the year Adam had chosen to suddenly become interested in girls? How could he, with everything else that was going on?

At the sound of a familiar laugh, Jenna turned her

head and saw her sister and Marissa dancing with a bunch of the guys in the corner. They were busting out their best club moves, even though the Texas Reel was playing over the speakers. The guys clapped and hooted, and Marissa and Stephanie looked like they were having the time of their lives.

Adam was getting to know Alyssa, and Stephanie was dancing up a storm. They were both having so much fun. Why was Jenna the only Bloom kid who seemed to be miserable? Didn't they care about their family at all?

Soon, Adam and Alyssa were dancing and laughing it up with Simon and Natalie. Tyler came over and grabbed some punch for Stephanie so she could cool off. The two of them bent their heads close together and whispered and laughed as they sipped their drinks. Finally Jenna couldn't take it anymore. Everyone was having fun but her. And there was only one thing she could do to change it.

Decision made, Jenna waved to Chelsea, who grinned wickedly, nodded, and headed out through the kitchen. Jenna dropped the ladle and tromped outside. It was time to pull the prank of the year—maybe even of the decade. It was time for Jenna Bloom to truly make her mark on the Camp Lakeview social.

"Omigod! Aaahhhhh! Snake!!!!"

"What is nibbling on my foot? Hey! Is that Snowball!?"

"Get it away from me! Get it away from me!!!"

Jenna and Chelsea doubled over laughing in the

corner as the animals from the nature shack took center stage at the camp social. Now *this* was fun. Rabbits, squirrels, snakes, iguanas, turtles—everything but the fish and the birds had been released amidst the dancing, stomping feet.

"This was the best idea you ever had," Chelsea told Jenna.

"Couldn't have done it without you!" Jenna replied.

Ten minutes ago Chelsea and Jenna had snuck into the nature shack, using the extra hide-a-key that Roseanne kept in a fake rock by the door for those mornings when she was spacey from lack of coffee. Chelsea had seen her use it once during her time in the nature elective and had remembered the exact placement of the fake rock. Once inside, Jenna and Chelsea had each grabbed as many cages as they could handle and raced through the darkness back to the rear door of the mess hall kitchen. After three trips they had stacked up almost every cage in the shack and the animals were running around inside their pens, twittering and clawing and raring to go.

"Okay. Let's turn this in to a real hoedown," Chelsea had said, crouching in front of one of the bunny cages.

"Ready?" Jenna had added, her heart pounding. "One . . . two . . . three!"

They both opened the doors to their nearest cages and . . . nothing happened. Brownie the mouse just looked at Jenna with his beady black eyes. Snowball the rabbit ran to the back of his cage and crouched there.

"No, silly! You're supposed to go out! Out!" Chelsea ordered.

"Come on," Jenna said coaxingly. She reached in and picked up Brownie in her hands, then placed him by the door of the kitchen. "Run! You're free! You're free!"

The mouse started looking for crumbs.

"Maybe they just need some friends," Chelsea said.

So Jenna and Chelsea ran around, opening every cage in sight and dumping the animals out on the floor. Then, working together, they wrangled them toward the door, grabbing Leaky the lizard as he tried to make a break for it and giving Todd the turtle the nudge he needed. Finally . . . *finally* . . . the animals got the picture and, following Sandy the squirrel's lead, they fanned out into the mess hall.

Now, campers had scattered everywhere. Girls clambered up onto the snack tables, knocking over bowls of Cheetos and plates of brownies. A first-year girl screamed and launched herself toward the punch bowl, splashing the contents all over Stephanie, who was running to help. Stephanie screamed at the top of her lungs.

"Omigosh! Look at my sister!" Jenna cried, grasping Chelsea's hand as Stephanie's flattened hair dripped red punch onto her dress. Her mascara was already running, and she looked like the ax murderer from some bad scary movie.

"Check it out!" Chelsea shouted, pointing.

The Frodo Boy from the meeting was running away from, of all things, a chipmunk. He looked terrified as he ran out the front door and ran off screaming into the night.

"This is the best!" Jenna cried, beyond proud of herself.

"Everybody, calm down!" Dr. Steve said into the microphone. "Counselors and staff, please try to wrangle the animals!"

Pete dipped to the floor and swooped up a snake that was slithering toward a huddled group of senior girls. Daphne grabbed two of the iguanas and held them against her, cooing to them with a gentleness Jenna had never thought the girl could produce. Nate came running out of the kitchen, loaded down with buckets and boxes to try to contain the creatures. In every corner of the room there was screaming and chaos.

"Omigod! Somebody get the rabbit! The rabbit is getting away!" a second-year girl screamed from her perch on the DJ table.

Jenna watched as Adam tore across the room and grabbed Snowball, the white rabbit, by its haunches just before it slipped out the door.

At the sight of Snowball's panicked eyes, something inside Jenna's chest dropped, hard and fast. She hadn't thought of the fact that the animals could get away. Suddenly it seemed like all the creatures were scampering for the door, terrified by the screaming and running and crying.

Crying? Who's crying? Jenna glanced around the room and saw Marta, the girl from bunk 3A, standing with a drenched Stephanie bawling her eyes out. Julie was on the floor next to her with a Band-Aid and a wet cloth.

"What happened?" Nurse Helen asked, appearing on the scene.

"It was Rocco, the guinea pig," Marissa said, lifting the little pink-nosed animal in her arms. His eyes were darting around wildly. "He got scared and bit her ankle."

Nurse Helen pressed a piece of gauze into Marta's wound and when it came back all bloodstained, Jenna almost fainted.

"This is great!" Chelsea said as the chaos continued around them.

But it wasn't. It wasn't great at all. The animals were petrified and in danger. Marta's crying had sparked off a wave of tears among the younger girls. Everyone was miserable. And it was all her fault.

For the first time in her prank-filled life, Jenna knew immediately that she had gone too far.

chapter

TWELVE

"I'm very disappointed in you, Jenna," Dr. Steve said, leaning back against the front of his desk. Jenna had to tip her head back to see up into his face. He blinked rapidly, as always, but now it wasn't funny. His expression was so harsh—so serious. Before Jenna knew it, she was looking at the floor again. "I know you've always been a prankster. Your whole family is famous for it. But you've never done anything that caused injury or true harm. What were you thinking?"

I was thinking I was miserable, Jenna thought, sinking lower in her seat. *I was mad at my sister and my brother for having fun. I needed to do something.*

She wasn't about to say any of this to the camp director. It hardly made sense to her—how was it supposed to make sense to him?

"Is Marta okay?" she asked finally, her voice small.

"She'll be fine," Dr. Steve said. "Of course each of our animals have had their vaccinations, so there's no chance of rabies or infection."

Jenna let out a sigh of relief. If Marta had been mad at Jenna after Stephanie's reaction to the love-note prank, she must have hated Jenna now. But that didn't really matter. As long as Marta was okay, Jenna could deal with getting dirty looks from 3A for the rest of the summer. It was nothing new.

"But that's not the point, Jenna. The point is, it took over an hour to round up all the animals. Roseanne was beside herself with worry," Dr. Steve said, getting up and pacing to the other side of his desk. "On top of which, the camp social was ruined. There are over a hundred campers here who are none too happy with you."

"I know," Jenna said, her heart heavy.

She looked out the window at the bright blue sky. Even from here she could see the colorful helium balloons that were tied up all around the mess hall, welcoming the parents to camp for Visiting Day. Car doors slammed and kids shouted as they greeted the families they hadn't seen in four full weeks. Shira raced around, playing the happy hostess. Jenna knew that back in her bunk, all her friends were putting on their best clothes, brushing their hair, getting ready for one of the biggest days of the summer. And where was she? Stuck in the director's office, waiting for her mom to come in for a meeting.

The prank had not been worth it. Not by a long shot.

Jenna wondered how many of the kids had already told their parents about the social. By the end of the day she *was* going to be famous—but in a bad way. Not exactly what Jenna had imagined.

There was a quick rap on the door, and Jenna's stomach turned.

"Come in," Dr. Steve said.

Jenna looked up to find her mother, brow wrinkled in concern, stepping into the room. Her curly hair was pulled back in a low ponytail, and she was wearing her favorite blue sundress and white sneakers. But her eyes looked tired and worried, and Jenna was instantly sorry for giving her anything negative to think about today.

Out of habit, Jenna looked for her father to step through the door after her, but of course, he didn't. It was like there was a big empty hole where he should have been.

"Jenna," her mother said. And Jenna was out of her chair like a shot, hugging her mother as tightly as she could. Jenna had no idea how much she'd missed her mom until that very second. "Honey, are you okay?" her mom asked. "Shira told me to come right to the office. Is there anything wrong?"

"I'm afraid we have to have a serious talk, Ms. Bloom," Dr. Steve said.

Jenna looked up at her mom, who looked back at her with that disappointed expression that Jenna knew so well from other after-prank meetings. She felt like she was about to cry. "I'm really sorry, Mom."

"It's okay, baby. Just wait outside while I talk to Dr. Steve," her mom said, running her hand over Jenna's hair. "I'll be right out."

"Hello, Mrs. Bloom," Dr. Steve said as Jenna slipped through the door. "And will Mr. Bloom be joining us?"

Jenna closed the door before she could hear her mother's response. She dropped down into a chair in the deserted waiting room, closed her eyes against her tears, and waited.

"Let's go for a walk," Jenna's mother said when she stepped out of Dr. Steve's office. She was clutching her purse, and her mouth was set in a thin line. This was not a happy mom.

Jenna stood up quickly, her knees shaking almost as badly as they had on the diving pier. "I'm not kicked out of camp, am I?" she asked.

"No. You're not kicked out of camp," her mother said, opening the door for her with a loud creak. "Though I have to say, I find that decision surprising after what you pulled."

Thank you, thank you, thank you! Jenna thought, practically skipping out into the sunshine. Even though her mother was clearly upset with her, Jenna couldn't help being relieved that she wasn't going to have to go home. There was no way she could have handled living for four summer weeks at that house without her brothers and sister. They may have been annoying to have around camp, but she would need them at home. Especially with everything that was going on.

Jenna and her mother stepped onto the main drive where Pete and a bunch of the counselors were directing parents to parking spaces. There wasn't a paved lot at Camp Lakeview, so they made do with a wide expanse of dirt and did the best they could to fit in all the cars. The tires kicked up a lot of dust, and Pete and the guys were using the bandannas from last night's social to cover their mouths while they coughed.

"So, do you want to go find Stephanie?" Jenna asked brightly, hoping to change the subject.

"Eh! You're not getting off that easily, kid," her mother said. "You are going to be punished for what you did last night."

Jenna's heart fell. She had known this had to be coming, but she still didn't want to hear it. "What's my punishment?" she asked as they turned their steps toward the picnic tables at the edge of the woods.

"You'll be getting up early every morning for the next two weeks and helping Roseanne feed the animals and clean their cages," her mother said.

"Every morning?" Jenna blurted.

"Yes. Every morning," her mother replied. "And if you ask me, Dr. Steve is going lightly on you. This is the least you can do to make up for that ridiculous prank."

Jenna tucked her chin and tromped along, her hands hanging heavy at her sides. She knew what she had done was wrong, but that didn't make taking the punishment any easier.

"Jenna, is there anything you want to talk to me about?" her mother asked, dropping down on a bench at one of the tables. She hefted her large purse onto the grainy wood and turned her intent gaze on Jenna.

Suddenly Jenna's insides squirmed. "Like what?" she asked, sitting next to her mom.

"Like why you did this?" her mother asked. "I know you like to play jokes and mess around. I know you have a free spirit. But you're a smart girl. This wasn't a whoopee cushion or a trick pack of gum. You couldn't have thought this prank was harmless."

"I know," Jenna said quietly.

"So what made you do it?" her mother asked, reaching out and running her fingers through Jenna's hair, untangling it down her back. Usually Jenna loved her mother's gentle, comforting touch, but after everything she had done, it just made her feel worse—like she didn't deserve the attention.

"I don't know," Jenna said, knowing it was a lame answer.

"Well, let's think about it," her mother said, still combing. "What were you thinking about just before you let the animals into the dance? What were you feeling just then?"

Jenna flushed at the memory, her heart twisting in her chest.

"You can tell me, Jen," her mom said. "You know you can tell me anything."

"I was . . . I was mad," Jenna said finally. She stared at her sandaled feet, kicking out one, then the other, from under the bench.

"Mad at whom?" her mother asked gently.

"At Adam. And Stephanie," Jenna said.

"Your brother and sister?" her mother said, sounding surprised. "Why?"

"Because they were having so much fun!" Jenna blurted, finally looking at her mom. "And I don't get it! I don't get why they get to have so much fun while I'm so . . . so . . ."

"So what, Jenna?" her mom asked her.

"So sad!" Jenna half-shouted, a tear spilling over onto her cheek.

Her mother's eyes softened slightly, and she wrapped an arm around Jenna, pulling her to her side. Suddenly Jenna was crying loudly, pressing her face into her mother's shoulder to hide in case anyone happened to walk by.

"You're sad about me and your dad splitting up?"

her mother said quietly.

Jenna nodded into her mom's arm and sniffled. "And no one else cares! They all act like there's nothing going on! They act like dad is still going to be living there when we get home. Like . . . like everything hasn't changed!"

"Oh, Jenna, I'm sure that's not true," her mother said. She wiped Jenna's tears with her thumbs and smiled down at her. "Everyone reacts to this kind of thing in his or her own way. Are you really telling me that neither of them—not Adam, or Stephanie—has acted any differently this summer?"

Jenna sniffled again and thought hard. She thought about Adam and how he had tried to talk to her a couple of times about the upcoming divorce—how she had avoided talking about it. And come to think of it, Adam *had* been spending a lot of time taking pictures and sitting alone in the darkroom, when in the past he had been as active and athletic as Jenna was. Plus, Stephanie was even more mothering than usual this year. Maybe each one of them *was* just dealing with their family's troubles in a different way.

"I guess," Jenna said finally. "I guess they have been acting a little weird."

Her mother sighed and looked out across the camp, watching as parents hugged their kids and walked off with them to tour the grounds. Jenna wished she were one of them. She wished she was happy and excited and rushing her mom and dad to meet her friends, like she had on every other Visiting Day. Jenna was sick of being upset.

"I'm sorry this is so hard for you guys," her mother

said. "I wish there was something I could do to make it easier."

"I know," Jenna said sadly. "I'm just sorry I made it harder for you," she added, thinking about Matt's letters and how he had warned her to not get into trouble this year. He had been trying to protect her parents because they had enough to deal with: the divorce, her father moving. But instead of helping him protect their parents, Jenna had made things worse.

"Oh, sweetie!" her mother said, kissing her quickly on the forehead. "Please! I'm not your responsibility. I'm supposed to worry about *you*, not the other way around."

Jenna smiled slightly. "Well, okay, but I promise I'm not pulling any more pranks this summer," she said. "You're not going to get one more freak-out phone call."

"Freak-out phone call?" her mother asked.

Jenna laughed. "Long story."

"You're a good kid—you know that?" her mother said, reaching out to hug her again. "A little nutty, but generally good," she joked. Jenna grasped her mother tightly and closed her eyes. Everything was changing. She wished she could just stay here, hanging on to her mother forever, and that the rest of the world would just go back to the way it was.

"Hey! Look who's here!" her mother said, releasing her.

Jenna turned around to follow her mother's gaze, and her jaw dropped. There, walking toward her with her brothers and sister behind him, was her dad. He had a huge grin on his tanned face and was carrying a picnic basket bursting with food.

"Daddy!" Jenna shouted, running to him. Her brother laughed as she nearly tackled her father to the ground, but she couldn't help it. She was so surprised to see him—to see them all together—that she could hardly control herself.

"Hey, Boo!" he said, planting a kiss atop her head. He handed the basket to Stephanie and put his hands on his hips. "I have a bone to pick with you."

Jenna's heart skipped a beat. Was her dad mad about the prank as well?

Her father pulled a folded copy of *The Acorn* out of his back pocket and opened to the list of awards.

"Now, I really think you should stop winning so many events," he said. "It's just not fair to the other kids."

Jenna laughed as her dad ruffled her hair and draped his arm over her shoulder. Stephanie and Adam greeted their mother, and they all gathered around the table.

"Hello, Christine," Jenna's dad said, nodding as he sat at the other end of the bench.

"Hi, David," her mother replied with a small smile. "How was your drive?"

"Fine, thanks. Yours?" he asked.

"Great. Such a beautiful day," her mother replied.

Jenna exchanged a look with her siblings as their parents made small talk and unwrapped various sandwiches from the basket. It was weird, having them sit so far apart—having them talk to each other like strangers. But at least they were here, together. Things were definitely going to be different when Jenna got home after this summer, but maybe they wouldn't be as horrible as she had thought. She had imagined that her parents would never want to see each other again, that they would never be sitting all at the same table together like they were just then.

So her family wasn't perfect, but they never *had* been (especially not with Adam as part of it). Now they were just going to be a different kind of imperfect. Maybe, just maybe, Jenna could get used to it.

"I know what Jenna wants," her father said, opening the waxed paper around a white-bread sandwich. "A little peanut butter and banana?"

"Ugh!" her sister groaned as Jenna happily took the sandwich. "You're such a freak!"

Jenna took a huge bite and smiled a peanut-buttery smile. "I know," she said, her mouth full. "I like me that way."

And she meant it. However imperfect her family was, however imperfect *she* was, Jenna liked her life. From this moment on, she was going to start remembering that.

chapter THIRTEEN

Jenna sat in the darkroom that afternoon, determined to get at least one picture right before her two-week elective was over. Her parents had left half an hour earlier, after showering their kids with food and new clothes. Jenna had watched them talking as they'd walked to their cars, and even saw them hug good-bye. She knew enough to not hope that her parents were getting back together, but at least it seemed like their divorce wasn't going to be nasty and full of fights, like some of the divorces her friends had lived through.

"How's it going over there, Jenna?" Faith asked. She was working on her own pictures in the corner and now she looked up and checked her digital watch. "There's only about a half hour more of free time before dinner."

"I think it's going okay," Jenna replied, though she was at a total loss.

"Well, if you need any help . . ."

"I'll ask," Jenna assured her. But she didn't want to ask for help. She wanted to prove she could do it on her own.

Just then the door opened and in stepped Adam

from the curtained area outside the darkroom. He glanced in Jenna's direction and closed the door quietly. Great. Had he come to mock her photography skills again?

"Hi, Faith," he said.

"Hey there, Adam," she said, not even looking up from her work. Apparently she was getting used to having him around all the time.

Adam weaved his way around the tables and took the stool next to Jenna's. "Hey," he said, looking at her supplies. "How's it going?"

"Fine," she lied. In the twenty minutes she had been in the darkroom she hadn't printed one good picture.

"So, was Mom pretty mad about the prank last night?" Adam asked.

Jenna glanced at Faith, but then realized it didn't matter if they talked about it here. Everyone in camp knew she was responsible for the Great Animal Escape, which was what Pete had called it that afternoon.

"Not really," Jenna said. "She was cool about it."

"That's good," Adam said. He started lining up her film strips on the table, organizing them for her. "I mean, she probably would have been *really* mad if she knew what else you had done this summer."

Jenna froze. "What do you mean, what else I've done?"

"Oh, you know, the sugar in the salt shakers . . . that picture you took of Stephanie," Adam said. "You know, that was a nice shot. Maybe you should just stick to Polaroid. It's more your speed."

Jenna was too stunned to even whack him on the shoulder for the insult. When had Adam figured out that she was behind the other pranks? "What do you . . ."

Jenna stopped when Adam gave her an "oh, please" look. He was her twin, after all. He knew her better than anyone. There was no point in trying to act all innocent around him.

"All right. How did you know?" Jenna asked, her shoulders slumping.

"Well, first of all, the salt shaker thing was just like the trick you played on Uncle Earl last Thanksgiving," Adam pointed out, shifting on his stool. "You remember? When you put apple cider in the gravy boat?"

Jenna laughed. "Right! And he didn't even notice."

"Said it was the best gravy he'd ever had," Adam said with a smile.

"Aunt Jo did not like that," Jenna said. "Okay, so maybe the sugar prank wasn't the most original idea I've ever had. But what about the Stephanie thing?"

"Well, you and I are the only ones who know about that gross mask thing of hers except for the girls in her bunk," Adam said with a shrug. "I knew it wasn't me, and all the girls in her bunk worship her . . . so I figured somebody had to talk them into it. Who else would do it but you?"

Jenna let out a little whistle. "Wow. You're good. Maybe you should become a detective or something."

Adam grinned wickedly. "Why do you think I'm so interested in photography?" he said. "P.I.'s make tons of money, you know."

Jenna was struck for the millionth time by how much her brother's thoughts were like her own. Back when she had decided to take photography one of the reasons was so that she could learn to take spy pictures of her family. Clearly Adam was thinking along the same lines.

"So if you knew all along . . . why didn't you tell on me?" Jenna asked.

"I don't know," Adam said, toying with a lever on the exposure machine. "I guess I just figured . . . you know . . . we already had enough stuff going on. I didn't want you to get in trouble on top of everything else."

Jenna's heart squeezed, and for the first time since she was about five years old, she felt like hugging her brother. She resisted the urge, though. It was just too weird. He probably would think that she was taping a "Kick Me" sign to his back.

"Is . . . is that why you've been hanging out in here so much?" Jenna asked him, looking down. "Because you're upset about Mom and Dad?"

Adam shrugged again. "I dunno. Maybe. It's just weird hanging out with the guys and trying to have fun when all these bad things are going through my mind. It's like one second I'm laughing and then all of a sudden I remember that Dad moved out and I don't really think anything's funny after that. Would you believe that Eric and those guys actually started calling me Adam-Moody? Like it's all one name. Adamoody."

Jenna laughed at the joke, then covered her mouth. "I totally know how you feel," she said. "It's like one second I'm happy and the next second I'm yelling at people. No one's given me a nickname yet, though."

"Huh," Adam said, his eyes wide. "You really do know how I feel."

"Yeah. I do," Jenna said. She felt about a million percent better to know that her brother was going through the same emotions she was.

"Wow," Adam said, looking as surprised and relieved as Jenna felt. "We should have talked about this ages ago."

"Tell me about it," Jenna replied.

They sat there smiling at each other for a long moment. *Huh. Maybe Adam's not so bad after all*, Jenna thought. And somehow she knew he was thinking the same thing about her.

"So, you want me to show you how to do this or what?" Adam asked, sliding closer to her.

Normally Jenna would have gotten all defensive if Adam, or anyone else, had forced his help on her, but for the first time all summer, she felt calm. She felt like she could deal with the fact that she wasn't good at photography. She felt like she could, and should, ask for help.

"Yes, I do," Jenna said. "I really, really do."

▲ ▲ ▲

The next day, Jenna trailed behind the rest of her bunk on the way to free swim. Ever since the Great Animal Escape all her friends had been sort of cold to her. They weren't ignoring her completely, but they weren't being all that friendly, either. The very idea of sitting by the lake on the outskirts of their crowd made her cringe. All she could do was hope that they wouldn't be mad at her forever.

"Hey, Jenna! Wait up!" Marissa called out, jogging to catch up with her. As always, the CIT was perfectly coordinated with a red bathing suit, red flip-flops, and a red-and-white striped plastic bag full of magazines and suntan lotion.

"Hi," Jenna said, surprised that Marissa wanted to walk with her. The CITs, especially Marissa and Stephanie, had been looking forward to the social more than anyone else in camp. Jenna had figured they would be madder at her than the rest of the campers.

"So, how's it going?" Marissa asked, her ponytail swinging back and forth as they walked.

"Okay," Jenna said, pulling her towel more tightly around her body. "Except everyone hates me."

"Everyone does not hate you," Marissa said, slinging her arm over Jenna's shoulders. "It was just the camp social. Half the people there didn't want to be there, anyway."

"Really?" Jenna said.

"Please! You remember what it was like when you first started here," Marissa said. "All the younger kids don't know what to do at dances, whether they're square or otherwise. And, you didn't hear this from me, but all the CITs want to do is sneak off and smooch somewhere," she added, lowering her voice.

"Oh, ick!" Jenna said, sticking out her tongue with a laugh.

"All I'm saying is, people will get over it," Marissa said. "You'll see."

Just then, Marissa tripped forward a few steps and Jenna caught her arm.

"Stupid flip-flops," Marissa muttered. One of her red sandals was lying on the path a foot back, having slipped off. "Hang on a sec, will you? I want to put on my tennis shoes."

"Sure," Jenna said, following Marissa over to a rock so she could sit. Jenna didn't see what the big deal was. The lake was about fifty yards away, and Marissa could definitely make it without changing her shoes. But Jenna wasn't in any hurry to get to free swim, anyway, so she waited, watching the other campers laughing and chatting as they streamed by.

Marissa pulled out a pair of white tennis shoes and shoved her feet into them, then placed the flip-flops back into her bag. She retied the knots in her laces and finally stood up.

"Okay, all ready," Marissa said, dusting herself off. They started toward the lake again, side by side. "So . . . you think you want to try diving again today?"

"I don't know," Jenna said, feeling that familiar pit of fear start to form in her stomach. "Maybe I could give it a try . . ."

Her words trailed off as she and Marissa came to the end of the pathway and stepped onto the sand. There, directly in front of her on the beginners' diving pier, was her entire bunk, along with Tyler, Stephanie, and Adam. They were all lined up on either side of the platform like they were forming a runway.

"Let's go, Jenna!" Stephanie cheered. Everyone clapped and shouted and called out her name.

"Omigosh," Jenna said, stepping to the edge of the pier. "What are you guys doing?"

"We're helping you dive," Tyler said, stepping forward and walking her to the edge of the platform. "This whole scaredey-cat thing? It's definitely not you."

"You think?" Jenna said.

"Come on, Jen," Stephanie said. "You're the bravest chick we know. I mean, what you pulled the other night might have been totally beyond stupid— ow!" Adam had nudged Stephanie in the side to get her to stop talking. She rubbed her ribs and continued. "But it takes guts to do stuff like that."

"Yeah, if you can coordinate the Great Animal Escape, you can totally dive," Natalie put in.

"Not that we're saying you should ever do anything like that again," Julie put in. *Ever.*"

"Don't worry. I am all pranked out," Jenna assured her.

"Come on, Jen," Marissa said. "Do you really want to be standing on the planks all summer, or do you want to dive in and join the rest of us?"

Jenna stepped up to the edge of the platform. Maybe it was because her heart was so full, thanks to her friends and family for supporting her. Or maybe she just didn't care anymore. But either way, the fear was barely there anymore. Marissa was right. It was time for Jenna to take the plunge. It was time for her to do something really daring.

Jenna stood with her toes hanging over the edge of the pier and raised her arms over her head the way Tyler had taught her. With all her friends, her counselors, her brother and sister cheering behind her, Jenna grinned, took a deep breath, and went for it.

Turn the page for a sneak preview of

camp CONFIDENTIAL

Grace's Test

available soon!

Dear Emily—

Hey there, chiquita! What's up back in Boringtown, U.S.A.? I bet you've been spending the whole summer just lying by the pool, right? I'm having a blast here at Camp Lakeview, as if that's any surprise! My bunkmates rule—they're almost as cool as you. (Calm down, I said almost!) I'm in the same bunk as Brynn, Jenna, and Alex again, which is so much fun. It's hard to believe I haven't seen them since last summer—we just slipped right back into our old friendship. I'm lucky to have so many friends here. Not that they'll ever replace you, my bestest friend in the world! I wish you could come to Lakeview, too. It's weird being best-friendless for the entire summer. And I know you're probably mad at me. I'm sorry I haven't written yet, Em, but you know how it is. I keep meaning to, but then—

Whatever. I haven't told you the most amazing thing. One of the new girls in my bunk, Natalie, is the daughter of Tad Maxwell!! Can you believe it?? He came to Lakeview with his girlfriend one day during the first two weeks, but he couldn't make it for Visiting Day last week. If only my parents were famous movie stars so they'd be too busy to get here for a visit. But no, they showed up. With about five more books for me to read. Ugh. They spent the whole time lecturing me, as I'm sure you can imagine—

Grace Matthews sighed and put down her pen. Her best friend, Emily, deserved a letter. She'd already sent three letters up to Grace at Camp Lakeview, and Grace hadn't answered even one. But it took so long to write a letter . . . and there was always so much fun stuff to do at camp. She glanced around bunk 3C at all her friends. Sure, some of them were writing letters, but lots of them were busy doing more interesting stuff. Well, except for Chelsea, who seemed to be doing nothing but staring at herself in her hand mirror. Grace liked Chelsea well enough (even though she could be bossy sometimes), but she thought that it must be pretty boring to spend all of your time looking at your own face. Grace shrugged and turned her attention to one of the other old-time campers like herself.

"Hey, Brynn," Grace called down from her top bunk. "What on earth are you doing?"

Brynn stood in the center of the small room, her feet planted about ten inches apart on the scuffed wooden floor. She was bent over at the waist, her arms hanging down and her short dark red hair falling over her face. She'd been standing like that for at least two minutes. "It's yoga," Brynn said, her voice muffled. She was speaking into her knees, after all. "My mom gave me an article on Visiting Day about how lots of actors do yoga to keep themselves focused."

Grace grinned. She loved acting, and she knew Brynn did, too. In fact, it was the only real interest Brynn had. "Mind if I join you?"

Brynn shook her upside-down head. Grace jumped down from her bunk, took her place next to Brynn, and copied the strange position.

Hanging head-down wasn't so great, though. All the blood rushed to her head, making her cheeks and her neck feel hot. Her curly red hair was longer than Brynn's, and it kept getting in her eyes and covering her face. She moved to pull away a strand that had gotten caught in her mouth, but Brynn protested. "You're supposed to keep still," she said. "Don't move, just pay attention to your breathing and to the stretch in your back muscles."

"That's right, Grace, don't forget to breathe," Jenna Bloom said from across the room. Jenna put on a slow, deep voice as if she were trying to hypnotize someone. "Breathe in . . . breathe out. Breathe in . . . breathe in some more," Jenna said in her "soothing" voice.

Grace couldn't help it—she got the giggles. "How can I pay attention to my breathing when I can't breathe?" she asked. Leaning over like this made it hard to take a deep breath, and she felt herself getting a little dizzy. She stood up quickly and got a head rush. "Whoa," she cried, stumbling backward. Luckily Marissa, bunk 3C's CIT, was there to catch her.

"I'm not sure you're mellow enough to do yoga, Grace," Marissa joked.

Brynn stood up very slowly. "It's a shame," she commented. "You could be such a good actress if you tried. Yoga could really help you be more centered."

Grace decided to ignore her. Brynn's whole goal in life was to be a famous actor, and she could never understand why Grace wasn't as focused on that as she was. But to Grace, acting was just something fun to do. She loved it—she *totally* loved it—but mostly because it was easy, and she was good at it, and it gave her a chance to be someone else for a few minutes. She didn't need to be famous or anything. She just loved acting. Whenever things got tough in school, acting was her favorite way to escape from the pressure. But none of her bunkmates knew that. None of them had any idea how it was back at school. Summer camp was for fun, not stress, and that was exactly how Grace liked it.

"There's no more time for yoga now, anyway," Marissa said. "Dinner's ready. I just came back to grab my hairband—I forgot it." Marissa snatched a pink elastic from her cot and took off, letting the screen door bang shut behind her. She and the other CITs were responsible for serving the meals in the mess hall. If you could call them meals.

"Okay, everyone, let's go chow down," Julie called.

"You don't have to tell me twice," Jenna joked, heading for the door. She was so athletic that she spent lots of time eating—she needed plenty of fuel to burn out on the soccer field.

"I think it's spaghetti night," Alex Kim said. She rolled her eyes at Brynn, her best friend. "In other words . . ."

". . . cardboard strips in tomato soup," Brynn finished for her. They both laughed.

Grace had to admit, the food at Camp Lakeview wasn't gourmet. In fact, it was even worse than the cafeteria food back at school. But eating every night in the noisy mess hall surrounded by all the other Lakeview campers was enough fun that the food didn't matter.

She climbed down the two rickety steps from the cabin and followed her bunkmates along the path toward the mess hall. Natalie and Alyssa walked right behind her.

"I didn't even get to dance with him," Alyssa was saying. "It's no big deal."

"But he obviously likes you," Natalie replied.

Grace grinned and turned around to walk backward so she could talk to them. "Still talking about the camp social?" she asked. "It was almost a week ago!"

Alyssa shrugged, making her orange-red hair swing. She'd dyed it that color the night before the social—by accident. It was supposed to be red, but something had gone horribly wrong. Grace was secretly a little relieved not to be the most Ronald McDonald-like girl in the bunk for a change. But on Alyssa, the strange color actually looked good—sort of punk. Alyssa was so artsy that she could make anything weird seem stylish.

"Adam was totally flirting with Alyssa at the social," Natalie said. "And I know she likes him, too. She's just being shy."

Alyssa stuck out her tongue at Natalie. "And *you're* just trying to make us forget about you and Simon," she teased.

Grace laughed. It was true, Natalie's relationship with Simon had been the big topic of discussion in bunk 3C for the past few weeks. Well, first it had been Natalie's famous father, and then Natalie's sort-of boyfriend, Simon. But for the past few days, things had been a little more serious in the bunk.

Grace glanced over her shoulder to check on where Jenna was. She was tromping through the trees at the head of the group, as usual. "Hey, do you guys think Jenna's doing okay?" she asked, lowering her voice.

Natalie squinted at Jenna's back. "She's been quieter than usual, I guess," she said. "But I think that's normal."

Alyssa nodded. "She's probably still embarrassed about the Great Animal Escape."

Grace shuddered just thinking about it. Jenna had always been a prankster—some of the best memories Grace had from last summer were of helping Jenna prank their rival bunk, 3A. But the night before Visiting Day, Jenna had gone too far. She'd let all the animals from the nature shack out of their cages . . . and into the camp social. It had been mayhem, and Jenna had gotten in a lot of trouble.

"Adam says she'll be fine," Alyssa said. "And he should know, he's her twin!"

"Oh, is that what *Adam* says?" Grace joked.

Natalie laughed, but Alyssa didn't even blush. She could be pretty impressive sometimes. When Grace had first met her, she'd thought Alyssa was shy because she was so quiet. But in the past month, she'd discovered that Alyssa wasn't shy—she just didn't see the need to talk unless she had something to say.

"It must be nice to have a twin," Natalie commented. "It's like having your own built-in best friend for life."

"Yeah, must be nice," Grace agreed. She turned back around to walk forward, and for the first time she noticed that her whole bunk was lined up in pairs. Jenna walked along chatting with Julie, who she'd known for years because her whole family had been coming to Lakeview since forever. Then Brynn and Alex, Sarah and Valerie, Alyssa and Nat . . . even Chelsea had a buddy. She was walking with Karen, one of the most timid girls in the bunk. That was a little weird, but the other pairs were totally normal. They were all best friends.

Grace felt a pang of homesickness. Well, maybe

not homesickness, exactly. More like *friend*sickness. She missed Emily. They'd been best friends since kindergarten, and Emily knew everything about Grace's life and her family and all her issues . . .

Why don't I have a best friend at camp? she suddenly wondered. *Everyone else does.*

The thought had never occurred to her before, and it was so shocking that she stopped in her tracks. How had she managed to spend a whole summer here last year without making a best friend? And she'd been here for half the summer this year without one, too.

"Whoa, Grace, did you fall asleep standing up?" Natalie laughed, pushing her gently in the back. "I almost walked right into you!"

"Oh. Sorry," Grace mumbled. Nat and Alyssa stepped in front of her, and Grace trailed after them.

"It was nice to meet your mom," Alyssa told Natalie. "She's more my speed than your father. No offense."

"Don't worry. Even I can't keep up with my dad's crazy life," Natalie replied. "But I always have fun with my mother. And she really liked your parents—she told me so."

"Yeah, maybe over the winter we can all hang out," Alyssa said. "Our parents can keep each other busy, and then we can get away with doing whatever we want!"

Natalie grinned and gave her a high five.

Grace sighed. If only her parents were the kind of people who she could have fun with. But they never even seemed to understand the idea of fun. Lately the only thing they did was give her lectures or "talks" or " suggestions." Even at Visiting Day, they hadn't wanted to talk about camp. They'd wanted to give her another lecture.

Snap out of it, Grace ordered herself. *Mom and Dad aren't here now. So I don't have to think about it.* She was here at Lakeview, her favorite place in the world, and she was going to enjoy every minute of it. Or at least she was going to try. It would be easier if she could talk to someone about what was going on . . .

Grace quickened her pace, catching up to Natalie and Alyssa. They were still talking about Visiting Day, but Grace's mind wasn't on their conversation. She just watched the two of them, walking along close together, teasing and laughing with each other . . . they'd only known each other for a month, and yet they acted like old friends. Best friends.

I can't believe I didn't finish that letter to Emily, Grace thought, horrified. What if her best friend really was mad at her for not writing all summer? Grace had promised and promised that this year would be different. That this summer she'd actually keep in touch. The whole time, she'd known that Emily didn't believe her. Emily assumed that she wouldn't get a single letter from Grace, and so far she was right.

Grace took a deep breath. Of course Emily wouldn't be mad. Emily understood how hard it was for Grace to write . . . it took too long and there always seemed to be something more fun going on. Emily would just shake her head and laugh, because that's what best friends did.

A burst of laughter erupted from Natalie and Alyssa in front of her, and Grace felt a little flicker of jealousy. If she had a best friend at camp, she wouldn't have to keep this all to herself. She'd be able to talk about her parents' annoying behavior at Visiting Day. She'd be able to talk about . . .

Oh, never mind, Grace thought. *I have lots of friends here. And that's better than just one. Isn't it?*